the inactivist

the inactivist

chris eaton

INSOMNIAC PRESS

Cover designed by Jamie Lirette (http://members.rogers.com/yars)
Cover art by Ross Bonfanti (www.awolgallery.com/RossBonfanti.php)

National Library of Canada Cataloguing in Publication Data

Eaton, Chris, 1971-
The Inactivist / Chris Eaton.

ISBN 1-894663-53-5

I. Title.

PS8559.A8457I53 2003 C813'.6 C2003-904822-5

The publisher gratefully acknowledges the support of the Canada Council, the Ontario Arts Council and the Department of Canadian Heritage through the Book Publishing Industry Development Program. We acknowledge the support of the Government of Ontario through the Ontario Media Development Corporation's Ontario Book Initiative.

Printed and bound in Canada

Insomniac Press
192 Spadina Avenue, Suite 403
Toronto, Ontario, Canada, M5T 2C2
www.insomniacpress.com

prologue.

They made a bet...

...because money was how one spoke in this day and age.

...because competition was a way of living, and they had a little extra scratch to throw around, and they were just a little bit bored with their jobs.

...and because it was certainly the only way any of them would ever get in shape on their own. The Michelin Man. Grimace. The Great Root Bear. Who could lose the largest percentage of his weight in two months? Even when the Root Bear broke down after three days—discovered in the back storeroom bingeing on raw hot dogs and mayonnaise packets, frozen onion rings straight from the bag—no one could have foreseen the drastic changes that would overcome Grimace. He was never heard from again; so gaunt and gauzy did he become that he haunted the Playland like a rotting Chinese eggplant. McDonald's had to pull all their characters from advertising for years until they could re-fatten him up.

For the Michelin Man (i.e., Bibendum), not even money could help him. For once, it had accomplished nothing.

He weighed in at exactly the same amount, and went home to brood.

Things were not good. The world of tires was not the same as it had been when he started his company over a hundred years earlier, in Claremont, France, using an old family recipe to shape rubber into the first cushioned bicycle tires. With the victory of cyclist Charles Thery, the first and only competitor to use the new Michelin tire in the Paris-Brest-Paris race in 1891, suddenly everyone wanted a piece of the action. A year later, some ten thousand cyclists were using Michelins.

It was Bibendum's marketing sense, however, that made him such a success. The original creative copywriter. Before him, advertising relied solely on shock and wonder. Fear. Lies. Bibendum was the first to use hedonism and envy. Twisting the truth in the gut of the nation. If it hadn't been for him, the gasoline-powered automobile itself might never have taken off, hiccuping along on its solid frame wheels, moaning and cracking on the jar and plunk of each revolutionary pothole. In order to convince the Paris bus system to switch to rubber, he skidded the city with images of the *Gendarmerie Nationale* coming down hard on a crowd of protesters:

If Parisians get fed up travelling on buses with solid tires and want to enjoy a more comfortable means of transport, all they have to do is get arrested.

He'd practically invented the car, goddamnit. Not to mention road signs, travel maps, trains, airplanes, the first concrete landing strip. He designed the first car ("And it was electric, too! Back at the turn of the last century!") to break the 100 km/h barrier. In the First World War, he supplied the French army with bombers. Some, free of charge. They made the tires for the space shuttle.

He invented the freaking tire!

How quickly the world forgot.

It was no longer enough to put his word, his name, his face, on every product they rolled out. The competition was too stiff. Too numbered. Michelin was losing ground to Goodyear and Goodrich, with their anonymous presidents and expressionless babies; Bridgestone and Yokohama were closing in. At the International Tire Exhibition and Conference in Akron, Ohio, Bibendum bored them all with his tales of the old days, and they passed him by for the chance to drop things from the blimp, or flocked to take a photo with the latest brainchild of advertising genius Burningham Barnum: the Firestone Swedish Bikini Team. Rubber versus silicone?

How could he compete? When he rolled over at night, the grooves in his mattress were increasingly deep and filthy. The children who had once loved to play and dance with him now just teased and taunted:

"Beep, beep, beep,—yo, guy, watch out, wide load backing up…"

When they only made those tires for bicycles, he could still fit into his old high school sash. It wasn't until the French tyre-ant took his act on the road that he started loading on the spare tire. By then he'd also abandoned his French accent, the product of months of vocal coaching. His advisors suggested plastic surgery, but he laughed it off, all the while knowing they were right. He was weak. And image was tantamount to success. The fitness craze of the nineties had been hard on most of the spokes-industry. Most of the sugared cereal hawkers like Count Chocula and Frankenberry were out on the street. The rest of them—here, the Great Root Bear was actually a prime example—were hidden in disgrace.

Bibendum would have to suck it up, or likewise get stuck in the mud of obscurity.

The new look of Michelin. Smoothing of the facial treads. Laser eye surgery. The removal of the entire panniculus of fat at the stomach. And when it was finished, the residual air and rubber collected in balloons and GLAD bags around the outpatient procedural rooms, they would do what they did with all the other frayed rejects, recycling it into shoes for sweatshop kids in Marrakech and Dakar.

The doctor slid the cannula between the third and fourth tires of his abdomen, and the air wheezed out like an asthmatic bugle corps.

part i. summer.

On the second day, they told him (i.e., Kitchen) to screw the radio ads. Just screw them. Stupid fuckers. Clients missed their projection by 5%, only made 394 million instead of 404 million, so they were cutting all spending, firing most of the plant workers in Wisconsin, the ones they'd bought just a month ago, former employees of a competitor, some ploy to gain market share that never worked because the customers who were loyal to the old company never made the connection with the new one. "Why should they?" his Creative Director (i.e., Roast) spumed like microwave soup. Did the average consumer read the trades? waiting anxiously at the salt-stained newsstand for the new issue of *Channel Business*? *Computer Reseller News*? discussing the benefits of hot swappable component redundancy or greater Mean Time Between Repairs (MTBR) over hot swappable Eggo waffles and the smallest Mean Time Between Starbucks (MTBS)? "Christ on ice, Kitchen!" Meanwhile, all these corn farmers in Wisconsin, who never had a choice but to turn in their ploughshares for company shares, pounding the electronics assembly line because everyone knew the Canadians were constantly underselling them agronomically with their stupid friggin' government subsidies. Communists. Plus, who ate corn any more, anyway? Didn't have as much beta carotene as broccoli. *Or* Vitamin C for that matter, which the State of Florida had somehow masterminded into the be-all and end-all of vitaminry. ("The mighty ad dollar!" Roast was screaming, kicking back in his ergonomic chair, whacking his palm against the wall. "Are you listening to me, Kitchen? Are you? Here's ten bucks. He who spends the most money runs the world!") And who needed real corn when Green Giant and Birds Eye could genetically produce cob-less corn—*grown frozen for increased ice-crystallized freshness*!—in mass quantities for their own canned niblet line, for the specialty salsa producers, bleached and shellacked for novelty Halloween teeth? Their slow motion, black-and-white ads basically made the cob obsolete, played on public fears, appealed to the public's sense of environmental welfare. Shots of Iowan landfills grown hunched and menacing with "organic corn by-products" and "maizic waste." Stories about animals and young children getting cobs lodged in their underdeveloped throats and dying of asphyxiation, "the leading cause of infant death after homicide, car crashes, fire, drowning, SIDS, cancer, farming incidents and international terrorism." After severe lobbying from several children's rights organizations, the government nearly made it illegal to farm the stuff. And not even the elderly, who were most prone to nostalgia—who set up pickets outside the White House when the President made an offhand comment about the Internet finally replacing the radio, succeeding where television had failed—not even *they* were apt to oppose the bill, their dentures slapping against sagging gums, a constant reminder that they couldn't eat the stuff any more anyway. By the time people discovered that the cobs were actually good for something, were perfect for making mulch, pipes, abrasive hand soap, anti-stick agents, cardboard, industrial filters, chocolate bar nougat, molded furniture parts, nuclear waste absorbent, it was too late for the farmers. They might have stayed in business for themselves, given the crows free rein of the fields ("Who needs all this corn when the cobs is where the real money is? Hyuh, hyuh..."), and then shot the fattened scavenger rat birds for the KFC or the McNuggets.

But they'd already sold their farmland to the factory builders, to manufacture back-up battery systems for computers and servers.

Plus, Green Giant just started pumping out corn-less cobs, anyway.

Ho, ho, ho.

So here were all these Wisconsin ex-farmers suddenly out on the street, or whatever dirt pathway passes for a street in the middle of Ass Scratch, Wisconsin. None of their kids had gone to university. Why would you when there were plenty of good jobs right here in Necedah? They would train you on the floor, for Chrissakes! You'd have your first Ford before eighteen, hauling ass past the Dairy Queen, smoking-up across the street from the old high school ("Screw you, Filmore!"). The people who started this company, they were good people. Hired local. Gave to local charity. Not the newcomers. The usurpers. They moved the work south of the border. Probably never set foot in this town except maybe to boot the old man in the ass, smooch his wife, shit in his bed. When you're thinking about going public at year end, an old abandoned military outpost full of spics starts to look pretty good. You hardly even have to pay them. Instead of raises, you give the little grease-heads blue jeans. A pair of red tabs for undying Mexican loyalty.

"Would it be possible to boycott Levi's in protest?" someone suggested. But it was just as quickly shot down. Could they hustle around town in a pair of ass-fitting Gianfrancos or pleated Edwin Italian baggies? Calvin Klein purveyed an American "Everyman" look with his plaids and casuals, but he was also kind of fruity and inhuman. Did Jordache and Guess even make overalls?

So they had to swallow it like men. Rely on state unemployment insurance provisions or find another job. Maybe they needed people at the Screw Machine Company, or the National Wildlife Refuge. Or over at Livewire. That was practically the same industry. In fact, Livewire had been a supplier for some crucial components. And Bunker had a cousin who worked there as a supervisor, maybe he could get them all interviews...

And then there was Madison, or even Appleton...

Or, god forbid, Milwaukee...

Of course, with all these cuts, marketing was one of the first things to go. Not that the radio spots were expensive to make. They abandoned production values entirely, just plopped the scripts in front of the caffeine-sedated deejays and watched them rip off several hundred an hour. They were simply a symbol of frivolous spending, like an endless stream of pennies dropping in a political smear spot. "Frivolous?" Roast spun and pumped like a hydraulic top. "Give me fifty million bucks and I'll get you more than 8% market share!" He bunched himself tightly, performed small mental rabbit punches before exploding in all directions at once. "Give me fifty million bucks and I'll screw your pooch blue, if that's what you want. Are you listening to me, Kitchen?" He was. "Are you?" Yes. "Then what we have learned here is to collect all money up front. The buck stops here, there and everywhere. No one is to be trusted.

"Least of all the client."

And so it went.

Roast was a creative bluster of the new age, a staccatic asshole who danced to his own irrhythmic tune. When he'd first joined the agency, twenty pounds lighter but certainly no smaller, they'd tried to break his independent spirit with branding tradition, heaped all the established packaged goods on him. These were the companies that were too afraid of public opinion to try anything different, and large enough to get by with basic name recognition. Why try to grab the consumer's attention with expensive creativity when you already had her sudsing her delicates in your brand of overpriced detergent almost 75% of the time? The other 25%, she alternated with one of the other products you also made but marketed under a different name to create the illusion of competition. Why pay extra money for something spectacular when all you needed was the company logo to flash periodically alongside another smiling housewife, decked out in professional make-up for no one but her family (and/or the filthy dog, muddy paws hiding eyes beneath the table), closing every door and drawer with her childless hips?

Now that he was the Creative Director, Roast's office was practically a museum to laminate, every square inch of wall space lathered with the memories of his past glory. There were Budweiser ads featuring every washed up actor and sports figure imaginable ("Tastes great!" "Less thrilling!"). His first Clio Award. His second. Below the autographed photo of him shaking hands with Ronald McDonald, a snapshot from a Miramichi fishing trip with Sugar Bear (who chuckled when Roast asked him about rods and lures, as he perched over the edge of the river with his sunglasses riding the collar of his sweater, and reached his daily quota in about five minutes with two swipes of his manicured paws.) And a clipped still to commemorate the small part he played in the creation of the fabled 1984 Apple Computer spot (that part being he happened to work for Chiat Day at the time). Without the protective seal, those mementos would have long since disintegrated into the past, so quickly did the industry leave its elderly (i.e., anyone over forty) to drift away on swiftly decomposing flows of Gillette Foamy.

Is this mound of shaving cream thick enough to support this lovely ad executive...? Even after one take in the sun, the synthetic lubricating agents never looked quite the same, so they had to hose it down and build it up again. Thank god the whole mess was biodegradable.

Roast approached his client meetings like espionage. Or a poker game. Gathering information about the enemy while disclosing nothing. He wrote down everything, made pointless statements, sought out an agreement, and when he'd achieved a suitably vague sign-off, rumbled off to do what he pleased. He knew the one thing the product managers feared more than risking their image: paying more to protect it. *Well*, he shrugged, *we could go back and work out some new concepts, with a new strategy* (he unfolded the signed paper from his wallet, smoothing it out on the board table), but it would cost them. And as their heads began to subtly flutter with confusion, trying unsuccessfully to justify the cost of moving to another agency altogether, Roast went off to call the production team.

"Swan! Think you guys can recreate a full-scale Berlin Wall for under a hundred thou?"

There was the possibility, Kitchen supposed, that Roast still reported to some unseen tribunal of supreme Creative Directors, that he was a pawn just like Kitchen himself, kowtowing to this secret society of advertising undead: Volney Palmer and F.W. Ayer, pioneers of the biz, both kept alive more than one hundred and fifty years through constant application of Oil of Olay wrinkle remover and crushed Bayer aspirin. Perhaps even the more recent king of things, Burningham Barnum, great-grandson of Phineas T, the man who used careful postering to turn Johanna "Jenny" Lind into a North American star before she ever set foot on the New York pier. Through brilliant strategy and creative, and more than a few of his elaborate three-ring luncheons, his new agency had managed to land every single car and Internet startup account in the country.

What if each and every agency head on this deep-fried continent was just one more element in a self-sustaining plot, a way to convince manufacturers and corporations of advertising's necessity in the capitalist process? The real directors met maybe once a year in Philadelphia, site of the first North American agency Palmer started in 1849, to decide the fate of the world. Roast was just the lackey. A robotic, steam-headed proxy. Kitchen watched him bash his head against the wall, observed the way he paused, chuckled, moved on to tangentially opposed subjects, licked his lips, spat out a hair, thinking: *Roast, would you be prevented from harming me because of your prime directive? Were you frightened when they strapped you to the table and emerged from behind swinging doors with spinning devices that buzzed like cards in bicycle spokes? Were your dreams entirely rebuilt with your body?*

"Where is the scar from the chip in your head?"

Roast stopped in the doorway, wheezed like a wounded dog. "Give me back that ten bucks, you moron..."

They were happy, he thought. Or, rather, *he* (i.e., Kitchen) was happy and *she* (i.e., Trapeza) was less so, but kept quiet about it until she had another option in the wings. He was happy to have one less thing to worry about, to have a pattern of living to which he was familiar, happy to leave annoyances and mutual character flaws (she thought he was unmotivated; he felt she was lazy) unspoken, happy to masturbate when she didn't feel like sex.

Then, one night while watching her watch *Dawson's Creek*, she nearly turned to face him:

"I feel restricted by you."

...which was a new one, certainly a switch from, *You ignore me at parties*. Or, *I never know what you're feeling. You're in this shell. And you won't share things with me*. No...

"I need to assert my independence, to prove I can exist as a separate entity."

Hmmm.

"I've never loved anyone this much before..."

And it scares me...

And they had sex on the couch to sign the pact, one farewell fuck with the television still on, catching occasional glimpses of ads for home will kits (he stopped tonguing long enough to spit out, "Do they even know the audience they're targeting...?"), mattress sales, fitness, happiness. Attempting to prolong the moment, Kitchen tried to deny he'd ejaculated. "What are you talking about?" he tried to look shocked when she started to withdraw. "Where are you going?" But she could see it in his face, the flicker of his squintered eye, could feel him shrinking away.

So she performed a dismount, and retired to the bathroom to wipe herself.

"Fine!" he called after her. "If you don't need any more of this, so be it!"

Cos there were plenty of others who would want *this*, if she wanted to know. Squadrons of them. Surrounding the building as he spoke. A fabulous battalion of bulletproof amazons. Dressed in nothing but leather and olive oil. Ready to *descend* at a moment's notice, if she knew what he was getting at.

A panty raid. Porn troopers. The Poontang Clan. Har, har, har...

She turned off the water. "What?"

"Nothing..."

Kitchen wanted to leave on a high note, to encapsulate the idea of the perfect man, selfless ("Sure, you take that... What do I need a vibrator for?"). But he also figured this might be his last chance to come in her mouth ("It's salty... you love salt!"), or to coax her into a threesome ("But now there's no threat of jealousy... and Judith lives for this shit..."), and he swiftly fell from grace. Since there was a pretty good chance he wouldn't see another naked woman in years, he kept devising questions to ask her in the shower, breaking in when he thought she might be soaping up her tits, or bending over to scrub at her calves:

"Did you remember to call the hydro company to shut off the power...?"

"I'm sorry to bother you again... I just can't find the remote anywhere... do you remember where you put it...?"

"It's not there..."

"Found it... it was on the coffee table... right in front of me... feel like an idiot... yeah, I'll close the door now..."

"I'm making toast. Do you want toast?"

Roast dug deep to remove even the dirtiest, ground-in clichés and other creative traps (puns, simplicity, the dreaded "See & Say"). He was the Swiss Army Knife of Creative Directors, able to pull out the appropriate tool when needed.

Bring out the Roast and bring out the best.

You were in good hands with Roast.

The Agency was whiter than white, staffed with an under-aging team—even the ones who'd been there for decades somehow managed to retain their youthful ardour—of micro scrubbing bubbles. So many fresh faces. Whirling and foaming. Overpaid and undersupervised. Like an adolescent summer camp with unlimited desserts and no curfew. Swan claimed to have slept with over half a dozen campers already. Whee! Which made Roast the Bill Murray-styled counsellor, drinking beer with the kids, dropping sexual innuendo with whatever pills happened to be laying around. And when it came to crunch time, Roast was there to motivate, to help them rise to the occasion:

"You call this copy?"

Kitchen shrugged.

"I've seen better words in my kids' AlphaBits!"

Kitchen worked personally on the digital mini-tape manufacturer (shots of CDs hanging from rearview mirrors, used as coasters, rendered into mobiles and novelty Elton John glasses, to demonstrate the impending extinction of their usefulness), the Internet Movie Database (*All the useless information you'll never need to know*), the mobile phone service provider (*What* doesn't *give you cancer these days?*). For Crest, they took out advertising space in people's mouths ("FREE advertising space..."), reintroducing the blue and red triangles as the most omnipresent logo since the Nike swoosh, a cultural statement for the hygienically superior. Dentists were assigned strict criteria from the Crest for Kids Brand Manager ("You know, like, nothing falling out or anything..." "But they're kids..." "Yeah, and kids without teeth grow into adults without teeth. Is that the image we're trying to convey?"), and only the dentally unchallenged bore the mark of the Smile Creator, etched directly into the enamel with the same dye they used in Mr. Freeze. Of course, the real kick of the campaign came when it was launched in conjunction with Rosie O'Donnell's *For All Kids Foundation*, live on her afternoon talk show, after which the Tiny Tot Tooth Tattoos® became an even stronger mark of good parenting than the "*My child is on the Honour Roll at Small Town American Elementary*" bumper stickers.

The long-term effects were still unknown, so it was deemed to be safe. Like Nintendo. Or Kool-Aid.

It was a City with easily covered blemishes. They whited out the traffic problems by posting the viewscape with armies of billboards, entertaining swaths of six-word fiction, an ongoing epic that constantly referred to itself, communicated with itself. Most often it amounted to nothing more than branding warfare, like the Cola Wars, or the Beer Wars. But sometimes they rewarded the attentive driver with a concept that actually used the medium, like The Weather Channel's upward pointing arrows (*Told you so*), or the City Lens Factory, who placed a tiny, storefront sign by the road directly behind a mammoth magnifying glass (*We'll help you see anything better!*). Country Time Lemonade had launched a comeback as the continent's favourite summertime drink, taking advantage of the current heat wave, fabricating a Dali-esque billboard that threatened to spill all over the NBA sports stadium (named not after an ancient warrior of the court, of course, nor even the creator of the game or founder of the City, but after an airline company).

Then, they covered over the homeless and the tasteless shopping districts with a foundation mask of PR: Olympic bids and downtown art. "How do they even pay the *rent* peddling this dollar-store crap?" Roast perspired from between his teeth and lips. What had started as a simple sculpture project—each artist/company was given an identical fibreglass seashell they could decorate as their muse might dictate—had grown by leaps of logic and boundless hubris to become the *modus operandi* of the downtown urban planning committee. The hotshot young architect, Friederich "Lego" Blochs, had designed a waterfront that looked like an explosion in progress, the early seconds of a localized apocalypse. One side of the building (southern exposure, for more light) was entirely open, the iron threading of the concrete foundation like singed hair, curled and blackened, pieces of steel and glass debris somehow suspended meters away from the actual structure. The landscape around it was covered with realistic sculptures of downed trees and abandoned baby carriages, overturned luxury cars, with fountains made to look like broken hydrants. They shipped in dust and debris to give it that fallout look. People came from all over to see the thing, took photos of their kids and cousins and lovers and classmates spread out like victims on the floured waterfront pedestal, some shattering bottles of wine and lying down in the red pool for added effect. The Agency, among other hip young businesses, moved their offices there. And the builders filled the rest of it with shops and cafés. To ensure even more visitors. So they could justify raising the rents. Nothing like shopping to make a person feel complete. T-shirts and plush animals, postcards and snow domes, complete with post-apocalyptic ash. Hell, it seemed to be working pretty good for Disney.

How did you sell a city to someone? The object was to discover the Unique Selling Proposition (USP) and play it above all else. A place to spend your money. The rich couldn't very well live anywhere else. What would they do? It was the only place one could be truly successful. But of course everyone was successful, so it was all relative. The City was where things happened. The main selling point had to be its anonymity, where you could refuse to give money to the homeless and no one was the wiser; where small talk was no longer an issue because no one spoke; where you could date without expectation, and throw random verbal abuse without guilt…

The country was where you could get away from it all.

The City was a place you could be alone.

Kitchen could sell anything, even people. If someone were unattractive, he could sell him on loyalty. The shallow were honest. The small were not likely to be physically abusive. The stupid were often kind. You see a man in a coma? Well, I see a man who won't argue about the wall colour in the living room.

…

A happy man is one who's stopped making an effort.

…

He ought to have been able to sell himself.

When they first met, he forgot about it. And it wasn't until the third time they met ("Aren't you going to introduce us?") that she actually stuck in his mind, and suddenly they were in bed, because there was certainly nothing else to do in that town. She'd unfortunately landed a job in a nearby "small c" city as a staff reporter for a morning show: national, government-funded radio, like a home-schooled child who can only seem to relate to older people despite all attempts to be hip. He was without direction, so staying put seemed as good a choice as any. Trapeza made him feel joyous for the first time in years. And Kitchen liked to think he was better for her, too, although he wasn't sure exactly how. She was so foreign, concerned mostly with things that he'd always ignored. World affairs. Political scrums. International disasters, when and if they involved North Americans. He told his friends he was attracted to her because she was interested. Not *interesting*, necessarily, but *interested*. You know... in things. But what he really meant was that she was interested in him, that she would listen to his stories about old schoolground tussles ("I might have been small, but I was wiry..."), his days in the band ("When they found out what had happened, they held a benefit in my honour!"), or his meeting with the Pope, and never grow tired of them.

Then, after they had moved to the City and there were so many others to listen to, she grew tired.

Moving to the City was bad for Kitchen in other ways. He had always claimed he would like to take long walks in the forest, but in the City he wouldn't take a walk down the street. So Trapeza bought him a treadmill for Christmas because at least he could do that while reading his magazines. The magazines! Trapeza was afraid to go into a bookstore with him any more because she'd invariably find him berating some grad student employee for carrying both *Scientific American* and the *New Scientist* when it was clear that the *New Scientist* staff were just a bunch of hacks stealing directly from their competitor. Either that or they would fill their rag with sensationalist crap about "The Real Dope on Marijuana," an article on mobile phones called "Cancer Cells," or another theory on dinosaur extinction. He would draw the clerk's attention to an article on Sweden's time travel phenom, Dr. Ymer Framtiden (the cover story, no less, entitled "The Biggest Discovery: Of All Time!"), and ask him if he'd ever heard anything so ridiculous before in this life: "Is this *Amazing Stories* or something? Have I wandered unknowingly into a Star Trek convention? If I had a time machine, I'd go back and make sure this magazine had never been made!"

Before issuing him quite roughly out the revolving door, the security guard made him pay for the copy he destroyed.

But no one else was keeping up *their* end of the bargain. Weren't they supposed to make the world a *better* place? With magazines that were informative and entertaining rather than flashy and insulting? Seemed like you couldn't sell anything to men or women any more without a pair of tits glaring at you from the cover. *Cosmo*, *Maxim*, even *Time* had made the switch—under the guise of being politically correct—from *Man of the Year* to *Person of the Year*, almost immediately to *Woman of the Year*, and then finally to *Babe*, the first recipient none other than supermodel Micheline Burke. They stuck with the traditional head shot (even though the mere mention of it sent the young, male editorial staff into fits of snickering), but one of those new-age computer artists was brought on to assemble it out of a huge catalogue of cleavage shots, each one culled from years of swimsuit calendars and runway struts, tiny canyons of delight used like Lite-Brite pegs to form the greater image. Were these magazines not to be held accountable?

Trapeza was more than a woman. She was a mobile news unit. Her hair required careful editing, or else it went off in all directions like rumour. Her mouth seemed built only for the proper distillation of coffee. And she'd been working in radio journalism so long she'd grown a signal tower from the tip of her forehead, which she plucked each morning with vetting tweezers so that it was nearly unnoticeable. Through that satellite receptor she'd developed several beliefs and idiosyncrasies: her sentences were short and constructed mostly of verbs; nothing seemed important unless it involved citizens; she'd adopted a logic based on the Truth of deep, ovary-tickling voices.

"Were you listening to what the man just said?" Kitchen was trying hard to put at least one eye on her as he guided Lara Croft past the morphing statues. "He tells you that the head of the Taliban is Ben Hogan, and you don't think maybe it's a typo?"

She was enraptured. "Shut up, Kitchen..."

"This just in: Israel makes peace with Palestine..."

"Shut! Up! Kitchen!"

"C'mon, Trap, golf *legend* Ben Hogan?!"

How was she supposed to deal with this, the judgmental dismembering of each and every basic element of her being? He brought a flask of bad Canadian rye to her parties, not because he needed the extra alcohol, but because he enjoyed playing the part of the closet alcoholic, especially in a group of Hunter S. Thompson wannabes (the post-New Journalists, achieving realism beyond believability). He spilled the grainy firewater over his shirt in mid-swig, stepped on as many feet as possible, and then slipped into the closet or bathroom, neglecting to lock the door before raising it to his lips.

"Don't tell Trapeza," he would implore his discoverer. "She thinks I gave it up."

"..."

"Would break her heart..."

And later, on the subway home:

"I was just trying to fit in."

"Is that what you—? Arguing with my boss about how fact checking wasn't just asking three guys at the office?"

"My god, Trap, he thinks Crown Royal is a scotch!"

"And that sort of thing is so important...?"

"If you want to function in the civilized world, yes!"

"Civilization?" Is that what Kitchen wanted to call his sellout, spend-a-billy world? "Hawking brand names and insecurity to a market of social arseholes and mental invalids?" Did civilization amount to nine-to-five drinking, spewing nothing but marketable exhaust from between palsied teeth, each cash-addict as self-congratulatory as the next suit-wad...?

"Oh, please, when was the last time you saw me wear a suit?"

"What you don't understand, Kitchen, is the shallowness of your entire world. Other people... sensible people... *interesting* people... talk about world events. They discuss philosophies and worry about the future. All you people ever have to talk about is yourselves. The cars you're driving. The unaffordable house you just bought. And if it's not that, you're bad-mouthing other agencies because they stole your client, ohmigod, how did that happen, can't be that we treat them all with contempt, obviously someone must be blowing someone else. When I first met you, you wanted to write a book. You had a dream. You had things to say..."

"And fiction is a more— Jeezus! what kind of— You think writing experimental fiction for self-important grad school intellectuals is any more rewarding or worthwhile?"

"Is that what you— Kitchen, you never listen. At least not to me. You used to be better than the rest of them. You had dreams. You wanted to— it was just a way to make money. A private joke or some —I don't know—"

"Har, har, har..."

"But at some point, Christ, I don't even know what I'm saying any— shut up with that stupid— at some point you fell for it. Because the *cool crowd* at work accepted you. Look, stop it already. You *fell* for it. You started thinking their opinion was worth something, started thinking you were somehow—that you were better than me, started treating everything I did like it was some kind of pointless—Fuck, Kitchen, shut up with that stupid, fake laugh!"

"So what are you saying? That you're *better* than me? Because you know the names of powerless world leaders? Because your brain can log more useless trivia than a Thinkpad? Hello? Ben *Hogan*?"

"Kitchen, you think you— You can't just let things—" She wanted to look at him, couldn't look at him. "I don't know. I guess I just fell out of love. It's not like it was at the start."

"Like the start? It took me nearly two years just to decide I even liked you!"

"..."

"You think sexual attraction stays the same forever?"

"Shouldn't it?"

"You are *so* naïve."

"Fuck you."

"Serves me right for dating someone younger than me..."

The door slammed shut behind her.

"You should have done what I did, baby! Sleep around!"

Kitchen's creative partner (i.e., Miter) made a name for himself early by brainstorming the Band-Aid condom campaign. Johnson & Johnson had devised a condom with an adhesive strip to prevent slippage after ejaculation, swore it would lower the number of teen pregnancies, mostly because it would get them lots of free press but also because it just might, in that rare occurrence, help the one poor schmuck who wasn't sure he'd come yet. Miter worked on the concepts for weeks but came up with nothing, working his mind to the bone in taverns across the City. When Roast came looking, Miter fed him the slogan they'd been using for years.

I am stuck on Band-Aid brand, cos Band-Aid's stuck on me.

They outsold every other condom in their first week.

Miter had hair like a beach, full of sand, long yellowing reeds that seemed to stave off the erosion of the front hairline. But it hadn't always been that way. In older photos (shaking hands delicately with the marketing legend Burningham Barnum at the Clios; or at an office party trying to drink from a beer bottle shoved down the pants of one of his co-workers), his hair was short and dark like a suburban lawn, fenced in by collars and shirts that outsized his neck and chest, the occasional baseball cap worn at several angles. He had a distinct lack of an ass. He'd been forced to reinvent himself to survive in the business, and a dye job seemed the easiest place to start. Then he started going to raves, wasted in the neon-drenched corners, glow tubes stuck in his ears, as far away from the speakers as possible, his Dasani bottle filled with Bombay Sapphire. He tried Ecstasy briefly, tiny little dolphin-shaped pills that finally got him on the dance floor, but he dropped it when he caught himself making out with some high school girl behind the gym ("Wait a— Did you just say your *Home Ec* class?!"), unable to slake his thirst to be touched. His wardrobe seemed burned to his skin by a nuclear blast, futuristic and tight. His eyes were a pigsty, strapped with haphazardly tossed veins and mucousy debris.

Kitchen and Miter had been paired up almost immediately. No one would work with Miter. And Kitchen was the new guy.

Of course, everything really revolved around his kid. The club life was simply an image he portrayed to keep his job secure. Miter's wife Carla had wanted a child as soon as they got married ("Aren't you making enough?"). And now she was teaching the little slip how to read, how to tie his shoes. "How to be a better goddamn person, fer fuck's sake." Miter was just doing his best not to fuck the little shit up.

"You think I'm ready for this?" They were working on a pitch for Henckels knives, and he was trying to somehow balance the larger ones on their tips. The steak and paring knives were partially embedded in the far wall. He'd pinned a small stuffed frog to the board table with the cleaver. "I'm hardly thirty-five! I can barely masturbate without causing a fire."

"Maybe you should try to return it."

"Hmmm..." Miter was carving his initials into the bird's eye maple table. "By the way, I'm thinking something along the lines of 'well-balanced'..."

And Roast came crashing through the door with remnants of his lunch across his cheeks like a spiced rub.

"C'mon. We're going to The Tagline."

But outside the Agency, the world was unsympathetic and brutal, much less air-conditioned. They emerged from their exploding glass tower into the quick-foot and squiggle-heat (ouch, ouch, ouch!), poured themselves as quickly as possible into a chit-accepting cab (advertising cigarettes—*City smog causes cancer, too, and it's not nearly as Kool*—on both its crest and back seat), and tried not to sit back against the seats so they wouldn't develop sweat stains on the backs of their shirts. Kitchen was silent almost the entire trip, but Miter and Roast took turns pointing out particularly offensive billboards, then playing a game where they had to rime off slogans and advertising catchphrases beginning with the last letter of the previous:

"*That frosty mug sensation.* A&W."

"*Next to myself, I like BVD best.*"

"*The ultimate driving machine.* BMW."

"*Extinct is forever.*"

"You little rope snorter! What the fuck is *that* from?!"

"Friends of animals."

"PSAs don't count."

"Okay, *Even your best friends won't tell you.* Listerine."

"Shit..."

"*The greatest show on earth.*"

"Fuck you..."

"*Ugly is only skin deep.* Volkswagen..."

Kitchen had begun to dread these ventures into the outside world. Inside, they spoke with one voice, were part of a larger entity that *believed* in things. Simplicity was best. The image should lead the copy, or the copy should lead the image, but the two should never walk arm-in-arm like new lovers (the "See & Say," where words and image were redundant, as in showing a knock-kneed child with a caption like "*Time to go?*"). And Coke really *was* it, which is not to say that a paradox was created by Pepsi being the right one, only that they existed in harmony as co-number ones, one for sales and one in taste tests. Number one in the minds of the world. Number one for Generation Next. It just made sense! The damage caused by disposable Swiffer cloths to the environment was minimal compared to the protection they offered from common household germs and bacteria, viruses, the one true enemy, a tiny microbial arsenal threatening to bring down the entire capitalist system. Cigarettes were slowly killing the population, but their manufacturers were also great supporters of the Arts.

Outside, there were too many voices, each one screaming at him from the billboards and bus shelters, the storefronts and backpacks. He became disoriented, was no longer sure what he wanted. Out in this "real" world, the workaday, stumblerun, thinkandrest world, Kitchen imagined others like himself, or like those Wisconsin farmers, searching for something, wondering what it might be. Finances? Fame? Freedom? Someone else? ("Oh, Trapeza...") He'd always been taught to believe in himself, and he was quite sure he could accomplish his goals, whatever they turned out to be. But the real problem lay in their unearthing. With such a promising beginning (before he even walked through the elementary school doors he was already reading at a fifth grade level), how could one hope to progress in health and happiness? Everything was bound to disappoint by its very nature.

"Wake up, dreamboy. This is our stop."

And he followed Miter and Roast inside.

The Tagline was best read as a letter Z, scanning the back wall for the real big shots, diagonally to the prime booth to the left of the swinging doors (Swan had gone ahead, and fended off the other patrons with cardboard cutouts of Spuds Mackenzie and a pantyhosed Joe Namath), and finally to see if anyone was directly in front of you who might add another twist. Of course, there was rarely anything new and exciting. The entire bar was filled with copywriters and art directors, the walls covered with classic ads from the past, most of the older ones defaced by the current crowd to reflect the changing face of advertising. An old Beetle ad now bore the headline: *We can make you buy any old piece of crap*. A more recent poster for Apple had been doctored to read *Think ads*.

And they drank! How they drank! The beer ran like mountain streams, or large horses, dispensed by women in various costumes: amoral Loyalist settlers, in long skirts and corsets; blondes in pigtails and short Oktoberfest overalls, with corsets; babes in tank tops and cutoffs. Possibly corsets there, too. They rotated the taps every quarter to reflect the current advertising leaders, selected by a panel of Creative Directors like Roast for quality and inventiveness. Each one a product of near-identical recipes, tossing barley and hops with water and electricity. The only real differences were in the words and images they encompassed, or that encompassed them. The patrons ordered them by the names of the agency, or the creative team behind the thirty-second art flicks. Budweiser, made the most popular beer in America by Charles Stone III at DDB Chicago, became known as a Three-Stone ("Wassup?!" they called across the bar). Guinness's British BBDO-crafted import identity made it a Campbell & Carty. And microbrews, often pitched by agencies they'd never heard of, were rotated as the Art House of the Month.

Everyone was talking about the latest Citroën ad, an attempt to reintroduce the French getabout to American drivers through a spot called "Citroën Kane." Shot entirely in black and white, it both opened and closed on a close-up of a weather-beaten sign that read *No Passing* (an allusion to its supposed speed), then moved abruptly through several lighting experiments (shots of the car from different angles, extreme close-ups of the engine, a white cockatoo squawking loudly in the front seat, the shadow of the aerial cast long on the landscape of the hood) to a chorus line of women dancing round the new model, singing: "What's that name? Citroën!" With the manufacturer's name properly anglicized to rhyme with Kane. They'd even named the car the Orson to go with their new line of artist-named autos, a trend begun with the snub-nosed Picasso mobile shuttle. Quite possibly the best commercial ever made, although surely no one would ever buy it. Not in North America. Didn't look built for speed or for show. The socialist overtones were not so easily swallowed here. Plus (and this was a sentiment echoed by the Necedah crowd, leafing through the *Auto Trader* as a break from the regular job classifieds), could the French really understand complicated mechanical concepts like fuel injection and acceleration? Torque? Didn't they still use the metric system over there? Would the Orson be able to handle American gallons? No sense even chancing it.

About the only thing the ad had working in its favour was the soundtrack by the White Stripes.

In the corner, a group of rookies were etching their own words of wisdom into a Formica tabletop. In pencil! Roast snapped the offending HB in two, handed them his Mont Blanc, snatched it back, replaced it with his pocketknife ("Just because the product is fleeting doesn't mean the words shouldn't be permanent!"), which had Miter running off about the damn knives again, picturing the words *I ♡ MY HENCKELS* carved in just about any surface you could imagine, from cutting boards and trees to steaks and fish. ("Hell! Why not whole cows?!") On a completely different tangent, he drew a Henckels slicing and dicing a Ginsu (*Now, that's sharp*!). A gang kid refusing to play chicken with it. A fairly accurate caricature of Burningham Barnum with a devilish grin, handlebar moustache, and a beautiful lady on a spinning wheel (*Good advertising cuts through*). A joke, really.

"Or wait, wait a minute, shit yeah, we could say something like *The perfect gift for everyone on your list*. And then just show a wrapped present with a card made out to Michael Myers."

"Sign it Jason Voorhees?"

"Free hockey mask with every purchase."

They ridiculed those who had formed the industry convincing clients to focus on product benefits. Benefits? Every product was identical these days anyway, more often than not produced in the same factory by the same pair of hands. Advertising was all about branding, creating an impulse image of cool around a beer, speaker system, floor cleaner, microwave pizza. Backsides and belly buttons, tattoos and tank tops. That's what sold cars and carving knives. And even that evolutionary development of advertisers was going the way of the dinosaur. They couldn't rely on boobs any more. Couldn't make an ad flash its dimples at the consumer and expect the entire world to kowtow. The newest school was all about irony, the juxtaposition of old school with new school, high and low art. Campbell's finally using Warhol instead of the reverse; the appreciation of a huge Christo installation (millions of beach balls riding the crest of the world's largest wave pool) from the high-speed perspective of a new Z8; Gertrude Stein chugging Red Rose tea; hoooowheeee!

What could be more glorious? This jingly oasis! This haven for the metaphorically inclined! This island of spokespersonage! Who was that by the bar? Speed-talker John Moschitta? Having a practically unintelligible conversation about current smog levels with sports legend Bob Uecker? And all the unattractive people were almost invariably male, which made their mediocrity that more appealing. So, yes, bring on the girls! Was Kitchen ready for another relationship? Probably not. But did that prevent him from having a good time? No, sir. Any distraction was welcome. He'd had way too much to drink. Swan brought him a double Maker's Mark ("So, how's the girlfriend?" "Split last month." "Aw, geez."), and he danced with what he hoped was a girl (he was having trouble focussing, as well as measuring time) for what seemed like an hour. There was a girl named Butter smoking pot with some product manager outside the bathrooms, and Kitchen refused to give her any breathing space whatsoever: "But, really, what's your *given* name?"

"For Christ's sake, buddy, that *is* her name."

"I'm just trying to discover the girl's *raison d'être*."

"Leave me alone."

How was he supposed to find new companionship in this? in the basement of the Tagline, between this nursing student and her meddling friend, sucking this Big City weed that made him lose feeling around his eyes, nodding but not hearing? Swan was clapping him on the shoulder, spouting some nonsense about bucking up, telling him about a party he was throwing next week ("Art chicks, dude!"), but Kitchen couldn't really hear him over the jingles playing on the loudspeaker ("What? Artichokes?"), and left to find another drink. Only two weeks prior, he'd thought he'd found his perfect match, someone who was intelligent, attractive and interested. But when he called her a few days later, she refused to answer, and he discovered over the Internet that she was a fairly prominent lesbian in his community. That should have been the end of it, but he took some perverse pleasure in making her tell him. So he continued to call daily until she picked up.

"So what about that movie? You still gay-muh?"

"Not really..."

"You can't believe the reviews. It's the tobacco protesters. Anyone smokes a fag in a film these days..."

"Listen, Kitchen..."

"Practically rhymes."

"Sorry?"

"My name."

"I think maybe there's been a misunderstanding."

"I think I need a new throw rug. Do you like carpet? Hello?"

He was borderline suicidal, or at least overly dramatic. Unimaginative. Prone to considering "a world without Kitchen" at every non-active moment. In the shower. Drifting off to sleep. On the subway. When the Tagline bartender cut him off, he nodded slowly, rose with decorum, understanding, grabbed the first coat he could find, and spinning through the club's roadhouse doors (the fronts of two large Dr Pepper machines, the hinges stuck to the wall with Krazy Glue instead of screws), he turned quickly to pee on the steps. Fuckers. The sky, thank god, for the first time in weeks, was drizzling carefully on his face and hair, a light rain like Q-tips, wiping the pavement of its waxy soot. The rats and flies pressed brazenly from the porous alleys to lick at what little moisture they could find, and he opened and closed his umbrella like an iris exposed to a slow-pulsing strobe, unable to decide if he wanted to be dry or cool. Of course, when it was open, the whole world just went in reverse anyway, the rain coming at him from the sidewalk, or sideways shaken from the trees and bushes. It wasn't until he reached the old place he used to share with Trapeza that he remembered he didn't live there any more. He lay down on the subway tracks for a good twenty minutes before realizing the trains had stopped running for the night. What kind of City was it that stranded the chronically depressed right at the point when they were most likely to make up their minds about it at all?

"Damn your conservative budgets and urban sprawl!"

Of course, the rain stopped before the City could even roll over and acknowledge it, before it could get a good dosing on either side. The darkened patches of asphalt simply became another shade of dark. And the heat delivered one last roundhouse to the weak and fashionably inappropriate, those who'd been flying in the face of the weather forecast, deigning to exhibit long pants. Car and house alarms screamed in confused agony. On the north side, an elderly woman doused her knickers and pitched headfirst into the trash she'd just deposited on the curb. Legend had it that Colonel Sanders had similarly fried during a heat wave like this, not to mention Mr. Clean and Betty Crocker.

The bums downtown, meanwhile, were sticking to the plastic advertising booths where the buses were prone to stopping, left strips of their flesh on benches all along the main routes. The homeless shelters had to overstock with Vaseline to soothe and heal. The media salespeople had to personally hose the areas down every night so the advertising rates wouldn't go down. And the bits of shave-sliced ass meat slipped like processed cheese between the white bread grates of the sewer mouths. The entire City was riding on the backsides of its people.

Nothing felt clean.

He first considered something was wrong when he found the phone wrapped in tin foil. She (i.e., Trapeza) had bug-proofed the apartment, soaped up the windows, clipped the Internet cable. Kitchen ragged on the customer service rep for a full hour before they agreed to send someone by the place, and he sheepishly handed over fifty bucks when the technician waved the immaculately severed cord at him. And Trapeza performed routine inspections of the entire apartment building, particularly in the basement, behind the furnace, beneath the stairs, and in the super's storage cabinets. When Kitchen accompanied her on these late night raids, holding the flashlight as she ran her fingers along the cindercrete foundation, she would point to the slight discoloration around certain blocks, remarking on the fresh putty smell, the lack of period construction roughness. This, she claimed, was how they were getting in, tunnelling from the laundromat across the street. The perfect opportunity for surreptitious entry.

"Who?"

She shook her head, chiselled a small bit of mortar stone into a tempered phial, spat something about standard operating procedure.

"Why wouldn't they just do what the kids who smoke up on the roof do, and buzz every room until someone lets them in?"

Whenever he left the apartment, she looked at him strangely upon return.

The doctor said she was stressed. The pressures of drive shift radio had finally gotten to her. Always trying to sound confident and competent, pretending to be interested in things like house fires, mayoral elections, the endless environmental debate over the re-opening of the causeway gates; combing through the newspaper early editions for story ideas to use that afternoon. Why not? The papers were always stealing from them, weren't they? It was a cyclical food chain of journalistic cannibalism, examining every tiny event repeatedly from every possible angle until the next disaster or violent protest or bake sale for charity. As long as there was one single scrap left, they would gnaw on that gristly dog-choker till the cows came home. Maybe it was simply the radio waves themselves. All those invisible walls of sound travelling through the air at such alarming rates of speed, it couldn't be good for a person. The doctor said he'd read several cases in Med school about people shoving screwdrivers into their ears to get rid of the voices in their heads, convinced that the government could control them by playing with the dials, or issuing the proper combination of frequencies, layering messages until it came out like hiss but was registered in the mind as basic commands. Be happy. Work hard. Pay your taxes. Report your neighbours.

He'd even heard of people receiving radio signals in their heads from metal plates or braces.

He checked for fillings.

"I don't know what else to do…"

There was, however, nothing to worry about. She posed no threat to Kitchen or to herself.

Of course, you couldn't be too safe. So, right away Kitchen tossed the waterproof radio they had hooked up in the shower, broke the tuning knob on the stereo, bought a new alarm clock. There were several television shows that week focussing on suicide-proofing your home (child-proofing, actually, but Kitchen was nothing if not adaptable), so he bought plastic outlet plugs and fixed them permanently to the walls, replaced the gas oven with electric, threw out his Gillette and bought a used Remington. He hid the aspirin, the Tylenol, the codeine pills she hadn't used after having her wisdom teeth removed, even the Flintstones chewables. Could someone overdose on vitamins? Especially ones that were made for children? They were surely 50% sugar. Could you overdose on sugar? And what about birth control pills? The risk was too great. Flushed them all down the toilet when she was out mowing the lawn.

Jesus Christ! The lawn mower!

From that moment on, he insisted on chopping all vegetables, stopped wearing belts and ties, broke the garage door with that huge antique hammer he found at a garage sale for next to nothing, sawed the hammer in half, concealed the saw in the middle of his garbage so the trash collectors would take it away. They stayed home most nights because she was afraid of being followed, would waste too much time ducking down side streets to make the trip worthwhile. And it became increasingly clear (he caught her in the washroom trying to shove entire rolls of toilet paper, wad by wad, up the raw pucker of her ass, attempting, she claimed, her eyes watering with shame and enforced constipation, to stop the general deterioration of her body through waste) that he had to spend every possible moment with her.

But he couldn't exactly stop working, not with mortgage payments, car repairs, the laser eye surgery he wanted so badly.

And there was no way he could leave her, even if she'd gone loopy as the Trix rabbit, or that Coco Puffs bird.

He'd made a vow, for better or worse.

"But, K, not for *worst*." This from Miter.

"What would I be if I left her now? I mean, there's a word... no, there's an obligation..."

"You were *married*?"

"Well, that's, that is, we might as well have been."

"The Trapeza you loved doesn't even exist any more."

"No?" His head was performing figure eights, swinging on his neck like a confused ostrich. "No..."

"And all this crap about trying to help her, you think she even knows you're trying to help her? She doesn't even trust you to pour her coffee in the morning, won't let you walk behind her..."

"I love her... I suppose..."

"..."

"I just don't know what I'm going to do."

Then, miraculously, she came out of it. She'd been scratching at the door of the padded bedroom all night, Kitchen pressing his bulk against the other side, when suddenly she stopped, started crying. When he creaked it open enough to see inside without being poked in the eye, Trapeza was transformed, as if the depression and dementia were simple, physical attributes she'd shucked. Kitchen collapsed exhausted to the hardwood-patterned tiles, and she went to him and put her arms around him.

"Thank you," she cried. "Thank you so much."

But he'd been away from work so long, had learned to define his existence by her need for him. The first day she returned to work, Kitchen dropped her at the radio station, circled back to the apartment, and masturbated for the entire afternoon. He'd lost his drive, spent entire afternoons at the computer playing online video games, guzzling Coca-Cola, forgetting to call in sick. He became cynical and spoke to her bitterly, when he chose to speak to her at all. Kitchen could feel her crying herself to sleep—no noise, just that awful shake—but he couldn't seem to care, couldn't reach out to comfort her.

He just wasn't sure how to act around this new Trapeza. He wasn't the one who'd changed, it was her. And he was so afraid to act improperly that he receded into a state of total inaction.

He didn't come out of it until long after she'd run off with her Segment Producer.

When he returned to work, no one but Miter seemed to have noticed.

The City sky was never dark, never starry. The downtown core glowed like a neon fungus, with all those skittery club-hoppers and money-spenders, rubbing shells, swapping information on their tendrilled, business card legs. A group of kids lit a vagrant on fire and the executive class movie-goers threw money at him as they sashayed past, arms spread abreast in pure bravadic genius, roasting or toasting not the latest Oscar hopeful but the sixty-second spots that preceded it.

"Of course, the consumer will never get it. Brilliance like that?"

"Lost on them."

"We have to teach them."

"But one idea stretched over a whole minute? Worked better as a poster..."

"How sweet, Richard, a street performer, slip him a fiver."

The mock-homeless kids—just bored snots from the burbs—descended on the flaming bills, peeing on the oxidating gifts from above, and ran off with their pockets full of the charred, stomach-wrenching stuff, chased for blocks by a pack of territorial gutter dogs driven wild by the stench of hot piss. The casually dressed execs—ties balled in their pockets, dates hanging off them with Windsor knot fingers—let their crumpled parking tickets carom off the lemon-jellied curb and climbed into their SUVs for the short drive home. And Kitchen made off with a stray murder of coins, ducking through the crawling traffic to the waterfront, where he might at least find some semblance of home. Peace. A grey-yellow foam was eating slowly at the boardwalk supports. Someone had thankfully smashed most of the lamps by whipping their empties at them, and the white and brown glass scattered the grass like wild rice. A couple of men were fucking inside the large, hollow, iron head meant to commemorate something forgotten, and although Kitchen couldn't see them, their moans echoed out the cavernous eyes and nostrils, as if the giant goddess of the City were masturbating so slowly, so internally, so deeply, that it was imperceptible to human eyes. Kitchen used the change to buy a sausage, then was reminded with the first bite why he never bought them. He split the meat and bread evenly between the pigeons and the invisible beasts that roiled the lake's surface so close to land.

He spoke to his reflection in the water, leaning precariously over the seagull-stained railing, questioning existence, meaning, happiness…

Happiness? What was that? Where was fulfillment?

Certainly not in my job.

But in someone else?

Perhaps.

Screw that. He pushed himself away from the edge, tripped over an iron mooring cleat (or maybe one of those fallout tree sculptures), ended up flat-assed on the green. He lunged unsuccessfully at it with the heel of his boot. Twice. Something smelled like warmth. He was pretty sure he was lying in dog shit. Is this what it all comes down to? Lying on your back, brought to tears by horribly choreographed pop songs, with dog shit smeared between your pressed shoulder blades, or worse—horrible confirmation—the back of your head. The City wasn't, perhaps, the best place for him, after all. Trapeza had said it had turned him cold. Was she right? That he had changed? That his entire purpose was shallow and pointless? No, of course not. He performed worthwhile acts, kept the horny capitalist cock pumping away at the nation's slot, made sure no seed was spilled on infertile soil, inspiring the growth that made life worth living for the rest of those poor saps. Without people like him, the whole system fell apart. Without him, there would be no City, would be no news, would be no her, damn it.

Maybe I'll meet someone else. Someone better.

Not likely. Look at you.

But I have so much to offer!

Like what?

I guess you're right...

And he realized he was being watched from a shrubbed balcony by two obese Chinese children in their pyjamas, so he stopped. Kitchen pulled himself up using a nearby concrete bench. A small single-seater aircraft hummed by overhead, cleared for an island landing.

As deep summer passed into deeper summer, Kitchen was moved back to the UPS account, but he knew enough from experience not to waste too much energy on it. He researched the company extensively but wrote nothing, feigning disappointment when the next job was cancelled minutes before the deadline, blank pads filling his desk drawers like pristine Tic Tacs. Of course, he really wasn't accomplishing anything, just dwelling on the days Trapeza's hair had sometimes made her face more attractive than it was, the way it used to be, when it wasn't becoming bloated with long nights out, the way her hair never would have looked in this humidity, grown to outlandish proportions, smothering both of them. She woke with it pressed into her creased cheek and shoulders, the tuft at the small of her back growing darker with each day. Then, for some reason, she shielded her crotch with her hand as she made her way around the bed to the bathroom door. Eczema had stormed the beaches of her britches, established outposts behind her ears. The only exercise she was getting was occasionally jerking him off, and it was beginning to show in her arms.

When he'd loved her, these good days were the only way he saw her. It was the way he sold it to himself. On the bad days, the good days were superimposed, travelling along the dip of each hip, lingering on her smile and energy, the things that had attracted him to her in the first place. He saw only laughter, kisses, felt only whispers and longing and give. Her shyness ("Not now...") became endearing, more of a turn on, and he couldn't resist a reach-around when she was doing the dishes ("I said, 'Not now...'"), pulsing up against her, groping, crying. Then he gave up. She'd already given up. He started looking for things in her he would never miss. He began to wonder how she saw him.

When the heat refused to let up, he slept with the air conditioner off, to create the semblance of company, and his sticky thighs lifted off the spotted sheets as his toes bit into the mattress and his hand continued to pump. Thp, thp, thp. Calves like rocks, past a charley horse and on to come-filled paralysis, remembering the indirect whimper of her thin-set lower lip, how she reclined almost motionless, except to kick the sheets away, heating like a goddamn furnace. She never wanted him to touch her then, so blazed was she with her inner summer, his chest hair coiling slick and black on her chest and abdomen when he reared abruptly back. She shifted slightly, tensed her stomach as her hips presented themselves under her rump's delirious tuck. Then she went slack, shivered, giggled, laughing and sighing as she forced his entire body sideways, and he rose up for another go, brought to second arousal by the look in her eyes, the second entry so much easier, slower, lying locked together like that for minutes and hours.

Thp thp thp thp thp thp thp thp...

Once, with Kitchen pushing up into her because she'd stopped moving and he was almost there, she told him he was the first person she'd ever loved, how she never thought love was even possible, and how strange it was to have someone inside you who you never wanted to leave, just fuck all day like glaciers, or ancient turtles. He said, *You gotta love yourself first, baby.* But had he truly loved himself? Back then? With the bitterness of youth seeping through him like a fumigation? Was your "self" not just like your family? A character imposed on you from birth not by choice but by chance? Was there any reason why you should love that person any more than you loved the rest of the world?

And when the alarm went off, he showered and went to work. The subway track looked comfortable and inviting once again.

part ii. fall.

On the morning of his thirtieth birthday, Kitchen woke without an erection, the latest evidence of his failed life. He quickly reached down to fondle himself, eyes closed, trying to picture the new account girl from work or the supermodel Micheline, or Miter's wife, or even the girl from the Tagline who'd found him passed out on the floor of the ladies' room like a discarded Tampex wrapper. She had mump-like cheeks and tiny, crack-baby features. But the body...? Nope, total blank, couldn't picture anything but the shape of her foot. The toe of her steel-framed boot. She'd kicked the copywriter several times ("C'mon, prevert, I gotta pee...") before finally running for Security, and suddenly... What was this? Had they moved the entire party in here?

No small wonder, the floor so cool, so cool...

"I thought you said he was dead."

She pistoned hydraulically from the toilet trying to hitch her panties back down to a reasonably comfortable position. "Might as well be, man, the smell—"

"You didn't even check to see if he was breathing?"

"Like I'm gonna touch that old fart!"

And Kitchen was carried from the bar to Miter's new Citroën. "What's that name?" Kitchen was singing nonsensically.

In his porn film scenario, however, Crack Baby entered the washroom with her friend Wendy (there was something about those red braids), and the hastily written dialogue ensued:

"I think he's dead."

"You know, there's a reason why they call corpses *stiffs*."

"You're gross."

"Dare you to give him a blow job."

"OK."

And dropping to stubble-flecked linoleum <*cue music*>, raining knuckly kisses on the tip of his slumbering peter, gently easing the flimsy thing past her thumb-and-forefinger lips…

No use. The bugger wouldn't rise.

This was old age? They didn't tell you about this at university, no, you had to learn about the real life stuff from Bob Dole and Guy Lafleur, quietly whispering about "erectile dysfunction" when it seemed as though everyone else had left the room. ("Psst, now that we're alone, huh, let me tell you about my flaccid penis…") In the old days, Lafleur would have been beaten up by his teammates simply for letting a makeup crew fag him up like that, let alone confessing he couldn't produce the Habitant chub on demand. But advertising had broken down the walls of social interaction and discomfort. At least some of them. Sexuality. Race. The only barriers TV didn't seem ready to address were male hair removal (even though the Michelin Man and the Pillsbury Doughboy had both admitted to going through almost daily waxing to achieve their polished marshmallow shine), man boobs, the rotting of your stomach lining. In the mornings, Kitchen experienced terrible gas, like crust-piercing lava, or acidic Jello, or perhaps something worse, no doubt the residue of another hard night at the Tagline. But while the smell had always hung around like house guests, at least the waste units, until now, had remained distinct, solid and brown, even if randomly shaped and bulging like pottery made by spastics. Occasionally the logs were black from wine, or strangely, green from stout. When he dropped his load in the toilet that morning, blood started dripping from his ass into the bowl. The toilet paper came away red and accusing. Fuck. This is what happens when you don't treat your body like a temple! Ass cancer! He barely gave himself the time to dress before stumbling to the cab ("Just drop me off at the emergency doors!"), shoving people aside to get to reception.

"Sir, you're going to have to wait over there..."

"Holy god, I think I'm suffering from internal bleeding!"

The doctor made him take his pants down and lie on his side. Kitchen hadn't even bothered to do them up, so it was just a matter of rolling down the waist. There was a diagram on the far wall depicting the inner ear. Another meant for kids that anthropomorphized germs as little green men from old sci-fi films. Always wash your hands before eating. Don't stick your finger in your eye. Or your ear. Or your rear. Your ear. Your rear (har, har, har...). Approximately fourteen seconds of wondering how hairy his ass looked, and then he was yanking his pants back on over the hospital gown.

"The membranes circling your anus have recently undergone some serious trauma. That's where the blood is coming from. Not from inside you."

"Thank goodness..."

"Have you recently participated in anal sex?"

"He started telling him he hadn't had sex, any kind, in months, actually, then thought better of it. Who knew how well sound would pass through this slipshod budget-conscious hospital ventilation? "Yes, well, I... no..."

"Have you had any trouble defecating? Regular bowel movements?"

"God, I mean, holy...!"

"Then I might suggest you introduce more roughage to your diet."

But the discomfort didn't leave. The blood leaked steadily from the unseen wounds and swabbed his butt cheeks as he walked, irritating the skin through frictional irrigation. He moved like a strutting rooster, his ass stuck out behind him as though he planned to carry things on it. And eventually he just gave up walking at all, sat at home or took a cab.

At night he lay in bed resisting the urge to scratch, but as he drifted off the animal instincts took over and his fingers started prodding, beginning at the cheeks but swiftly moving to the problem's source, which only aggravated the irritation and increased the bleeding tenfold. He woke the next morning practically spraying from his rear end, checking himself in the mirror for new wrinkles and moles, whining about it over coffee with Miter. He was weak. He could admit that. But that's where the doctor should have known and stepped in, should have done something to save him from himself. Bandages. Salves. High-dosage sedatives so he could pass through the semi-comatose stage directly to REM sleep. Maybe some kind of cone, like the ones they used on dogs to keep them from biting a wound, only to fit around his waist like a hard-shelled skirt.

"Sounds pretty fruity…"

"Call it a kilt, then. Is that more manly? Jesus, help me, it burns!"

He (i.e., Kitchen) **didn't belong.** Not in this world. He knew it every time he rode the subway. When the car with the brown seats trundled by, he decided he had to be on it, ran to catch up, and then sat in reflective dissatisfaction, corner-eyeing the low mumblers and bag rustlers, the seat hogs and gum smackers, the ones who refused to wear deodorant, the ones who clipped their nails in public, men using their babies to strike up conversations with teenage girls, the other corner-eyes like him. Directly across from him, a couple trapped in their mustard-stained sweatpants, black T-shirts with faded team logos, matching mullets:

"What did you do with the Kools?"

"You spent the money on your new Adidas!"

"Well, that's too bad, isn't it?!"

Trapeza was right: how could he claim to be part of a society for which he had no real concern? In which, in fact, he barely participated? Moving from point to point within the same circle of co-workers? Instead, he'd become obsessed with the creative sell. He spent his days coming up with new ways to say the same thing. Over and over. *This kids' cereal will increase your imagination. Despite all your previous empirical experience, this microwave dinner tastes more like real food than ever. Our 4x4 will give you the illusion of being a healthy outdoorsman.* Was he seriously improving the lives of those around him? What had he accomplished by increasing the profit levels on what was already the leading brand? If anything, he'd simply made it affordable to introduce more layoffs.

His only consolation: the results of advertising were inconclusive at best. The latest *Scientific American* included a study by Johns

Hopkins University, in which they had secluded a dozen test subjects for several years (a new gimmick to get something back for scholarship money) without television, radio, magazines, newspapers, the Internet. The goal was to remove all ad conditioning, to reduce decision-making to an instinctual level based only on reason, tastes, primal needs, packaging. In almost all cases, the subjects were drawn to the same products that proved successful in the traditional market where advertising was so prevalent. They bought superior products, but recognized the value of a bargain. They spent no more and no less, attracted almost equally by impulse products situated at the cash. There was a strange increase, however, in the percentage of money spent on things like alcohol and potato chips. And they were drawn almost inexplicably to green boxes, bottles, cans, etc. The whole thing caused quite a stir in the community, until it was discovered the experiment was sponsored by Heineken. They were simply shifting strategy to go after the younger college crowd, coming in through the back door. After that, all the results were thrown out.

To do or not to do? That was the real question. Because even in his own neighbourhood there were causes he could have stood behind. The City was planning to tear down the outpatient hospital at the end of his street, for one thing ("Or maybe just a wing," he told Miter, "I'm not really sure."). The original building had been built in the late sixties when the government had been more concerned with getting buildings up than how long they would actually last, the cost of structural longevity certainly enough to prevent re-election. Without such strategic short-sightedness, how else could they continue to do such good things? To carry out their carefully designed four-year plans? To bask in the parasitic glow of the public concern? Besides, the old hospital was a Catholic institution. It didn't reflect the current neighbourhood face, and was religiously inconsiderate to the growing number of ethnic peoples, atheists and whatnots.

Meanwhile and meanwhile, out came the petitioners, with pens supplied free of charge by BIC. The pen maker's marketing department knew hundreds of hands would touch each shaft every day, would caress that plastic embossment (round stic *Grip* med. USA) like braille fetishists and think of BIC every time human rights were in peril, wherever "change" (the special campaign focus of the MVP Erasable™) was imperative. In their advertisements, they reenacted historically famous signings. Versailles. The NATO and Russia Act. The US Constitution (*"Hancock! Quit hogging the BIC!"*). And just like that, BIC had branded itself as the pen of the people. The question *Does anybody have a pen?* became the catchphrase of the entire North American continent, alluding to another fetish, freedom of speech, that one person—one body, no matter who it was—could not control the way we expressed ourselves. *Everyone* had the right.

The proper response: *No, we all have BICs.*

The Freedom of BIC.

Everything was about the spin. For the government, the goal in tearing down the hospital was actually to rebuild it. New and improved. The people deserved the best in facilities. The people deserved a place they could receive premium care without the premiums. The people deserved to have all their services streamlined into a well-oiled machine. But first, they had to rename it. And so far, Bayer and GlaxoSmithKline had emerged as the top bidders. Whether or not they would keep the Saint part was still under debate.

"Seems a shame to ruin the entire sign out front." The hospital's new PR director (i.e., Burningham Barnum, whose agencies represented all the front-runners) sharpened his teeth on the reporters. "Besides, at the rate these guys are saving the world from AIDS, anthrax and diabetes, won't be long before John Paul Two's giving them the old head ring to wear around, you know what I'm saying?"

Har, har, har.

In a televised press conference, Barnum unveiled the campaign's message (*Reflecting the changing needs of the community!*) with all the proper pomp and circumvention. Where the park was ("Heck, nobody uses parks any more, except maybe to smoke." A flash of the pearly whites. *Make 'em wait for it*, great- grandpappy always used to say. "And what kind of message would we be emitting as a hospital if we encouraged people to smoke?"), they would install a new detox unit. The larger recovery rooms ("Ten beds per…") would instill a greater sense of moral support and contagious camaraderie. And the new traffic pattern—they were moving the emergency entrance from the busy expressway to Kitchen's own street—was designed to make the citizens a part of the whole life-saving experience. "Lego" Blochs was brought in again to bring the "Reflection" goal to life, but his early models were composed entirely of mirrors, something the mayor found a tad literal for his tastes ("What? Is there no room for metaphor in art any more?"), and this gave local groups the opportunity to mobilize further (yes!), to come up with spins of their own (take that!). The homeowners were most afraid of drunks passed out in their own urine on the front lawn, and successfully turned the focus to "green spaces," a strategy that even managed to bring the teenagers on board, not to mention on to Kitchen's doorstep. BICs across America.

Here was Kitchen's big chance, his opportunity to make a difference. Here was this girl with bluish-green hair and a reddish-brown clipboard, a personal sense of expression (the hemp skirt he understood, but what about the blue leather Pepsi jacket, or the Gatorade satchel with the words *Is it in here?*), and a total expression of boredom. That and a neon Kool Ultra Light erupting from between her lips. He couldn't take his eyes off it. Bates Worldwide had run the campaign for Brown & Williamson, reintroducing the number three cigarette maker as "the kool young smoker's choice," starting with the *We built the house of menthol!* posters in mid-2000 (alluding to Kool's history as the first menthol cigarette but also to the rave scene kids were so into these days). They hired every kid in oversized pants they could find to paint the town green and white, pasting their mock rave pamphlets—featuring random photocopied images of dissected flies, lamps, bottles of milk, et cetera—to every telephone pole in the City; placed prominent spots in *DJ Magazine*, *Mobile Beat*, *Jockey Slut*; sponsored DJ competitions in New York, Boston, Los Angeles and San Francisco, as well as the DJ Olympics in Halifax, Nova Scotia; and even hired Paul Oakenfold, Fatboy Slim and Kid Koala (in the melee, the Chemical Brothers were snapped up quickly by Marlboro) to light a few up behind the tables. Brilliant, very underground, won every award in the book. And with the support of the advertising industry, they'd brought the whole thing out in the open, going straight for the peer pressure jugular, advertising in *Teen People*, *YM*, *Mad Magazine*. *Don't we all want to be Kool? Welcome to the Kool crowd. Your parents tell you not to smoke... but how Kool are they? What me, Kool?* Wow! The power of an idea! Not only had they brought Kool from number three to number two (no mean feat in this loyal nicotine world), but they'd also done it by increasing the number of smokers overall, something that hadn't been achieved since the major consumption drop of the nineties. They came out with these glow-in-the-dark cigarettes, nicotine-filled pacifiers, and possible plans to reintroduce Willie the "Mr. Kool" Penguin to a new generation of impressionable young adults.

"Look, guy, holy— like I don't get enough of this shit at home already, nobody paying attention to me and shit, jeez... Are you gonna sign this thing or what?"

"But don't you see?" He had her by the shoulders. "We're all paying attention to you! All you young people do is spend money! You're the major decision-makers in every family household. You choose the cars, the television sets, the home entertainment systems, my god—" He looked down at the clipboard. *We, the undersigned, reject the influence of corporate America on our homes and schools...* "Pardon me, but, where would you be without corporate America?"

"..."

She smiled uncomfortably, and the Crest triangles on her top incisors glared at him behind their faded yellow façade. She held the petition out again.

...

"Alright." And Kitchen signed his name as illegibly as possible before handing back the clipboard.

"But look, guy, yo, you forgot a couple spots, over here, if you just..."

"If I just, if I just— now she talks... Look, I just don't want to include my phone number and email address, if that's alright. I, um, get enough unwanted calls as it is..."

"Sure, guy, but hey— Like, the voice of the people can't be heard if the people are hiding behind walls, you know?"

"I realize that."

"So what's the point of having all these here signatures if I could have just made them all up myself, you know? If the government can just say all these here people don't exist cos they don't have a permanent address or even a way we can call them on the phone to verify?"

"That's a real question..."

"No, guy, like, sometimes you just have to stand up for what you believe in. Holy, this here signature of yours is like a faceless mouth, man, nobody's going to listen to it... No address? Do you know how hard it is for homeless people to vote? They aren't on any lists or nothing, and the idiots who volunteer at the polling stations won't believe them when they say they're citizens, like someone who looked that shitty and pathetic would cross our border and travel all this way to screw up our stupid voting process..."

"What if I told you I just don't care?"

"Don't care? I mean, c'mon, guy, what kind of heartless person are you? No wonder you don't have a phone number, like, who would call you?"

It was Miter's idea to start the Inactivist Group. A half-hearted shrug in the general direction of opinion. They wanted to tear down the hospital? So be it. In the end, how was it really going to effect Kitchen's life? Plus, isn't that why they elected politicians in the first place? To worry about these things for them? For that matter, why even vote?

"You know, if we all refused to do anything, we certainly wouldn't have problems like these. There'd be nothing to protest."

But wasn't that Kitchen's problem in the first place? What was it that had turned him so cold and unfeeling? The City? His job? When Trapeza first suggested breaking up, Kitchen took it like the man he thought he was supposed to be—the practical, thinking man—and did nothing to try to convince her he even wanted her to stay. Never told her how much she meant to him. Never offered to try to work things out. Just: "If that's the way you feel, baby…" Shrug. "Feelings like that just don't go away." In fact, he was the one who actually left the apartment first, lingering at the front door under a barren premise ("God, I know I'm forgetting *something*…"), hoping *she* might be the one to change *his* mind.

Out in the street, he took one last look back…

And she wasn't at the window.

Wasn't being callous the reason why Trapeza had left him in the first place? Before they split, she'd expressed strong interest in volunteering with children, teaching the underprivileged the finer points of news gathering. Social conscience. Proper enunciation. Sometimes half the task of rising from the lower ranks was just speaking properly. She'd gotten so much from her job, could still remember the first time she'd spoken to national news anchor Fred White, the original Man from GLAD (a natural occupational progression for a voice like that, with such rugged Marlboro-styled good looks) how it had affected her entire life. "I mean, I was on my way to becoming a team leader or something, or worse yet, a teacher." She wanted to be able to do that for some other little girl. She thought it might help her grow as a person.

"Yourself, you mean? Or the little girl?"

"Damn it, Kitchen, I just want to help people…"

"You won't even give blood."

The days and weeks passed with the same pattern, cuddled up in front of their hour-long dramas, scarfing their favourite junk food, Trapeza talking during the commercials, Kitchen speaking almost exclusively at the most important parts. Occasionally, a full-blown conversation would even sneak up on them:

"You think just because those things are made from rice that they're somehow better for you? That the rice somehow negates all the sugar and crap they sprinkle all over them?"

"And your Coke is some kind of protein drink?"

"It's *diet*."

"Aspartame is responsible for all the Gulf War soldiers contracting Alzheimer's, Christ, you'd think someone in advertising would be more aware of how some information is hidden in order to sell a product…"

"Learned how to use the Internet today? Did you happen to search for reverse advertising? Maybe you should think about who has the money to pay for all these aspartame studies. Nobody's impartial any more—"

"Can't some people just want to do good?"

"It's even kosher."

Kitchen could see something was troubling her, knew her silences better than her words. But inquiring might only bring it on more quickly. Plus, it was like opening an old paint can trying to get anything out of her. She stopped telling him about her day because, as she put it, "I spend the whole day talking, Kitchen, I mean, sometimes I just need a break, alright?" And he understood what she was getting at, had only asked in the first place to appear concerned, which was part of the problem, really, that he always found it necessary to pry so much, like, sometimes it was important for people to retain their individuality, you know, keep at least one part of themselves *to* themselves, grow independently, experience life through only one set of eyes. "Otherwise, things just get stagnant. Once people stop bringing things to the table, you have to move on or die."

In short, Kitchen was standing in her way.

"—and it's not that I'm saying it's your fault exactly, but it's something I think I really need to do and—"

"So do it."

"—not that easy, Kitchen, we have such a routine established, with the dinners we spend together and the sleeping and the television, it's like you always need me home at a certain time or you get all upset, and that's a lot of pressure for one person to bear—"

"Then talk to that friend of yours about it, whatsername, wasn't she helping kids learn how to dance or something? She must have some contacts or would know someone who could point you in the—"

"—can't explain it either, but for some reason being with you prevents me from, Christ, don't give me that look Kitchen this is just the way it is... This look, this... see, this is what I mean, how can anyone try anything *new* around here with that judgmental, oh, forget about it..."

Lord knew if she had actually gone through with the volunteer work, was probably still beating herself up about it, crying over starving African children on late-night infomercials, breaking down when she read about "the... I don't know... travesties... in Egypt or... someplace in the Middle East." Instead, she'd probably joined a gym, took up running, and found she really had no more time. It was either the kids or her ass. And if she was going to get into television later, well…

Well, he'd show her, would find some cause he could get behind. Miter started putting up signs around the office: *Who cares?*; *So what?*; *Don't vote for me*. They featured overweight men in sandals and wife-beaters, drinking beer on the front porch. Kitchen told him he wasn't interested.

"C'mon, that's exactly why you have to join!"

"Aren't you trying a little too hard here?"

"Jesus, you're right, I am, have to work out the rules…" He cleared the whiteboard, uncapped the marker. "Rule Number One: Nothing is worth it, live and let live, something like that…"

"Rule Number Two: Don't talk about Fight Club."

"No, I'm serious here, K, c'mon—"

Swan, on the other hand, was more than game. He'd had practice being inactive, in his artist days before becoming a production artist, living off government grants and tax evasion, writing off everything from movie tickets and cellphones to alcohol and condoms ("She was a gallery owner!"). At one point, Swan bought an old ice cream truck to transport his paintings from point A to point B. But he'd never once guessed that it would eat through so much gas, particularly as the price at the pumps continued to escalate. It also snapped the timing chain after about three weeks on a highway jaunt to the junkyard. Swan had the side door wide open, music loop blaring. And he was busy waving at a convertible full of college girls who were pretending to deep-throat Popsicles, when he suddenly lost most of his forward momentum. He threw the engine flap open, spit on the steaming mess, then crawled into the back to masturbate. He never drove the thing again. But when the gas station at the corner closed at three, he rummaged through the trash receptacles for discarded cash receipts (damn those new pumps with their automatic debit/Visa slots), then declared them as his own.

Even then, Swan was looking for the easy out ("Some way to get through life without having to live so much, you know?"), blaming most of his failure on his unwavering look of mediocrity. He was nowhere near attractive enough to reach the upper echelon, would never become a media darling, would never receive a sizable grant because he didn't know how to flash his dimples at parties. Nor was he ugly enough, like Roast, whose head sat on his shoulders like a boiling pot of creamed corn, or those lucky pricks with Down's Syndrome. With a face like that, you could walk into any gallery you liked, and the owner had to look at your stuff. Out of pity. Probably had to give you a show just to make herself feel better.

"It must be hard for you," she'd say.

And Swan would reply, "You don't know the half of it, sister."

"How did it happen?"

"Fire or something." Certainly not acne scars. But maybe a genetic degenerative disease, like in that made-for-TV movie where Ralph Macchio ages real fast. Or non-contagious leprosy? "Some bad disease."

"How long do you have?"

"A year, maybe. No. Make it a month."

"Your art shows such suffering. It's important to me that it reach an audience while you're still alive to see it."

"Haven't really loved a woman in so long, either…"

Even if he had just a really big monobrow. Or outlandishly large ears and hands. Or a harelip…

"I'm in," he said to Miter. "Where do I sign up."

It wasn't even a question. He was already looking for the clipboard. Miter put his head on his desk.

"Fuck you, Swan, don't you know a joke when you hear it, my god…"

"But I thought—"

"Too much thinking around here, not enough working— Do you ever wonder, Swan, what it would be like if we all stopped working altogether? Not so far off you know, with the robots and the supercomputers, Jesus, Kitchen imagine that."

"Like, everyone you mean? Or just us?"

"An interesting point, Swan, I may have to think about this one further, if you can just close the door behind you on the way out—"

"Miter..."

"No, K, I mean really there's a simple— okay, sure Swan, talk to you later... see you now... buh-buh— K, we can't ask people to sign up! Sign? Up?! They want to sign up, they're too keen for us. We just have to assume people are part of it and figure they're smart enough to catch on... hey, man, yo, Kitchen!"

Maybe he should become a big brother?

The months passed by like people you wouldn't care to meet. Not entirely without odour. But forgettable, at least. Kitchen had no idea it was fall at all until they mentioned it on the news one night. (Was that Trapeza on TV now?) All of his time was spent at home, or at work (where the surrounding trees were made from concrete), or in a cab somewhere in between, poring over the latest creative brief, taking a nap, checking his email on his Palm. By the time he realized what was going on, it was too late to actually enjoy anything. He asked the cabbie to drop him off a few blocks from home, but the leaves were already gone, not even left in the piles along the street where the citizens raked them, piled them, and hoped the City trucks would take them away.

In the fall, the City took on an entirely different character. Once again, the rain was looked on with scorn rather than as a respite. Quite justly. People looked down rather than at each other. And the taxicab industry embraced its prodigal public after a season of sun-worshipping and health-crazed walking. The cycle of life. Dogs and drunks peed all over the place and the smell hung around for days and weeks, small airborne puddles of aromatic filth that reminded everyone of death. Like the rotting leaves and buried gardens. People stopped to check the bottoms of their shoes, and sighed in relief at what they didn't see.

It was what they *couldn't* see that should have worried them. Outside the neighbourhood booze shacks and drug fronts, old men put a finger to the side of their collective nose, and influenzal clots hit the sidewalks with renewed fervour, like the first drizzly foreshadowing of the coming, coiling winter. The same people who raked the leaves—the shoe checkers—they dove for cover behind their echinacea and zinc (placed lovingly in little green bottles by Jamieson and Pfizer, the pharmaceutical Easter Bunnies), but the sickness clung to their salt-stained galoshes and mid-highs, was scraped along the carpet at home where the children played. And god knows the kids were into everything, kissing and licking every surface imaginable. Pretty soon the whole house was coughing and sniffling, puking and fevering. Kitchen did his best to avoid contact with anyone, but Miter picked up something from the keyboard of his home PC ("The kid's only five, sure, but Carla has him sending emails to her father or something, I don't know..."), brought it to work before the symptoms were readily apparent.

Yet another unstoppable force to be reckoned with. Like the communists. Or the ants that took over his apartment every spring. And Kitchen lay in his bed like wet grass, heavy and dew-streaked, wondering if it made more sense to move or keep still. When Trapeza had still been around, she would have gone to the store for Canada Dry, which was now being sold in drugstores as a children's cough syrup alongside the Robitussin and Triaminic (Barnum again, tapping into every mother's home remedy and every child's delight). No chance she'd hold his head while he threw up ("You know my gag reflexes, K..." "Yeah, I know." "...you'll have us both down there puking our guts out..."), but at least she'd hold him afterwards until the shaking stopped.

He made conscious decisions not to call her.

What was the point of even trying to fight?

Roast was particularly sensitive to this, this desire to reunite with Trapeza, in his own way: "Jobs and broads... You can't never go back..." By which he meant that it was time for Kitchen to stop thinking about the past and get on with his life, to throw himself back into the ring of emotional wrestling, stuff some mud in a few more g-strings. "Think you got nothing to offer? If advertising's taught me anything, it's that you can sell shit to an asshole. All you have to do is find the right angle, hell, do you think it was easy for McDonald's to market that cardboard paste to the tune of 100 billion served? But some lucky tit sucker came up with the idea to copyright the words 100% Pure Beef in the eighties, and it took people years to realize it has nothing to do with actual cattle content. Took them even longer to forget again…" He was pushing things off his desk onto the floor, trying to find a place to sit, and his hand settled on the latest *People*, started flipping through it. "But look now, my god, Tropicana's pulling the same stunt again, peddling the exact same concentrated crap as everyone else, only under the copyrighted disguise of 100% Fresh-Squeezed Florida Orange Juice. Christ on a trike, Kitchen, you just have to convince the asshole it's going to run out of shit eventually, and furthermore, when it runs out of shit, its job is pretty much down the can! You'll never see the stuff move faster!"

…which set him off on another one of his tirades about the current state of advertising in this country. This fucking country. Christ, the collective minds of most copywriters in this grammar-less nation couldn't string together a decent sentence. They thought being clever replaced being creative. Pandering to the lowest common denominator. Relying on dancing animals and geriatric hit songs to move their cellphones and family cars, their Wonder Bread and Cheez Whiz. And where were the *original* ideas?

Where indeed? Kitchen ought to have been able to sell himself. It was what he did for a living. And there were women, Kitchen surmised, who *were* his target audience. Artists with practical streaks. Businesswomen who enjoyed the theatre. Raised under strange religions to which they no longer professed attachment. Concern tinged with irony. Calves like Nike swooshes. Deliriously beautiful women upon whom he could impress some sort of brand identity not incompatible with his own.

But, of course, he was too close to the product, found himself difficult to market effectively. Every angle seemed too one-dimensional, or pretentious, or a lie. Any attempt at conversation came out watery drool, unstoppable and entirely flavourless. He was so used to sharing things so directly with Trapeza (any event, no matter how pointless), felt it when she succeeded, knew when she was angry or confused, almost intuitively. Instead, with a smile as awkward as a newborn bird:

"Pretty girl like you shouldn't chew gum."

"What? Man, like, who are you, I mean—"

"Makes you look like a cow, chewing cud like that, like your jaw is coming unhinged or—"

"—fuck off, guy!"

"Sorry, I was trying— I mean, forget—"

"Is that the way you normally pick up girls, holy…"

He also had trouble with context, which at its least nefarious meant he couldn't appreciate older films, could never acknowledge the breakthrough. At its worst, however, it meant expecting intimacy from the first date. And when it didn't emerge, he became discouraged and left off. Even with Trail, who seemed so right on paper, who vibrated like a tuning fork the moment he touched her, who did things in bed Trapeza would never consider. They spent nearly a month chewing through awkward dinners, coughing up sounds like laughter and interest, surprise, failing to touch, wishing they could just skip to the part where he lapped at her navel, or she huffed in his ear. In the end, she simply rolled over and started pulling the simple black skirt past her simple white hips, brushed her fingers quickly through her hair, and headed for the subway home.

"I don't even know how to explain it, really, it's not even that anything feels wrong so much… Just that nothing really feels right, you know?"

Which was the only way you *could* describe it. He'd invested nothing, hung out with her like a new novel, was entertained and laughed in all the right places yet was still unaware of her as anything but an object. A distraction. He stayed with her that long mostly because she was single, and he wondered if feelings might eventually develop out of repeated proximity. Of course, Kitchen didn't even believe in true love. This "no questions asked" policy of complete devotion and acceptance. He was practical, cynical. It was Trapeza who thought they had lost it, was sure she might find it in someone else again.

Then he met Gage.

Swan's Christmas party was a much younger set. His artist friends. "From before he sold out, you know, and went to work with you..." All piss drunk. Which was the only way they could stand one another, really. The university kids with their braggarty noisings, projected drunkages, hangoverisms in superlative degrees. The dropouts with their sullen looks and stolen beer. They eyed the window in the bathroom, with its easy access to the roof, and the dog, Adam, as if it might be fun, once again, to make the poor animal puke uncontrollably and then pass out embarrassed in the closet. The last time, it took Swan nearly a week to get the terrified dog back at his water dish. Swan had to feed him Pedialyte just to keep him from passing out.

The snow that winter was unlike any they had seen before in the City. At first it just settled like talentless buskers, doing nothing, expecting attention. But then, suddenly, just as the lampposts had begun to sprout their coloured lights, sheet metal bells and sleighs, the wind chafed at the downtown core and bled pure and white along the side streets and alleyways. The Mayor called it a national emergency. Called in the army. People got angry just to stay warm.

"Why can't we live in a civilized area, with seasons, or heated streets, or a weather-control dome?"

"Haven't you heard? They erected one of those domes over Antarctica. Then they decided it's more useful for scientific experiments to keep it cold. So they flew down another half-dozen generators to refrigerate it."

"I thought exploring went out with the abandoned space program."

"People still *go* to Antarctica?"

...which got them all started on the recent Antarctic expedition where the team therapist had become inexplicably depressed ("Who wouldn't? Not one good restaurant, I'll bet..."), and with no one else to navigate the perils of the human ego, the mechanic and the chef had to take crash courses in emotional freedom techniques (EFT), as well as goal-oriented thinking. They practiced first on each other, then on proxy Internet patients. And eventually they managed to bring the therapist back from the brink of indecision, navigating him deftly over the pitfalls of guilt and nostalgia. It took a team of Canadian pilots to airlift the overly emotive shrink to the Shetlands and then to Tierra del Fuego before he was introduced to the North American public on *Oprah*, a new expert on the debilitating effects of cold on the human psyche. The pilots flanked him on either side, mesmerized by the audience of American women, caught winking on camera more than once, their high spirits in direct conflict with the doctor's theories.

"So, you have to let us know, how did you manage to get Dr. DiSanto back from the edge of the world?"

"It's called a plane, eh?"

"Yeah. I flew it."

"And the world's round... No edge..."

Instant celebrity. The two of them were able to quit their jobs just by selling the film rights to their stories. No one ever heard from the mechanic and chef again.

"People still *come* from Canada?"

Miter stared at them from the acrimony of his alleged indifference. He and Kitchen had been screwed at work again. When the client decided to scrap the shoot they'd been preparing for weeks ("Do people who have the Internet even watch TV any more?"), Miter realized he'd get as much done doing nothing at all. He stopped working altogether. He spent his days playing video games.

And no one noticed.

Around the office, that was sufficient. Outside in the real world, it irked him to be surrounded by such wanton concern. Their heightened sense of superiority. Just because they had beliefs? Kids who couldn't possibly know any better, so young and opinionated, working up a thirst earlier that day in a rally against the cigarette companies, working so hard to be refined, exceptional, trying to make a difference. Trying so hard they'd forgotten to be interesting. They bragged to each other because no one else would listen, squawking about injustice and felons and courage and the dip. And about sneaking past security in underground tunnels, crawling through the smoke-filled pipes and vents, and dropping from the ceiling onto a board table attended by Dr. Willie Penguin, Joe Camel and the Marlboro Man himself, Philip Morris.

"Outside those office buildings don't look like much, man, cos they don't want us to know what kind of money they're really raping us for. Right? But inside it was totally decked out in *largesse...*"

Miter, who'd been eavesdropping from across the room, descended upon them like a police baton: "Do you even know what you're saying? Do you hear yourselves? Or do you just speak?"

"Jesus, guy..."

"Where do you *think* you learned that word?"

"Look, guy, I don't know what your problem is... but fuck off..."

"Maybe you just meant you got inside and discovered your girlfriend's large ass here."

He went outside to his car.

"Idiots..."

With the success of the cigarette companies, the gum hawkers struck back from both sides. They upped their donations to the American National Center for Disease Control and Prevention. Their new campaigns positioned themselves as the healthy alternative to smoking (*A habit guaranteed not to cause cancer!*). If the government was putting an end to smoking, they wanted to be part of it. But the Wrigley Gum Company also made a play for Monte Cristo cigars, lifting the trade embargo on the Cuban roller when they became 100% American-owned. *Hold your breath!* the banners flaunted themselves from the buses and billboards, *Monte Cristo is coming to America!* And Miter rushed out to buy as many contraband boxes as he could find. As the only Cuban cigar available legally on the market (*If you don't inhale, it can't hurt you!*), it was important to snatch up the entire old stock before they started stretching them with filler. Banana peels and corn husks. These kids could whine all they wanted about the world. But the greatest form of protest was to blow smoke in the face of controversy. He brushed aside the asthma-prone hippies to disperse his prize among the Agency contingent:

"Hey, did everybody get one of these— shit, Swan, it's not a goddamn horse bit, you don't have to chew the shit out of it, just light the damn thing and start puff—"

"You do things your way, Miter, and leave the rest of us alone."

"Fuck, I'm just saying your mother must have been in some pain with you as a child, man, have you ever heard of—"

"Look, just give me a light, will you, do this one thing for me or what?"

"Is that what you said to her last night?"

Har, har, har...

In the next room, a cellphone rang, and everyone started to giggle because it had been programmed to play an audio-pixel version of Herbie Hancock's "Rockit," which was still funny despite being so dated. The culprit was sitting on the gateleg beside the old-fashioned digital display model and this girl (i.e., Gage), on her way to confront Miter's creeping fog of non-conformance, and totally unfamiliar with technology of any sort, snatched it up like a free drink ("How do I talk? How do I talk?"), pressing every button she could find until the owner reclaimed it and it went suddenly dead.

"Fuck, you've even erased all my programmable numbers..."

"Oh, Gage..." (Practically in unison, as if she were the star of her own sitcom.)

"Yeah, right," she stepped to the centre of the room, where the lighting was better, and turned her face to the ceiling to express the taut wave of her neck. She was exquisite, innocent, energetic, youthful. "Look up 'gullible' in the dictionary and my picture's right there."

"That's what we told her anyway!"

She was so tiny when Kitchen first saw her, sat with her legs wide open, like a boy, elbows on her knees, head thrust forward. Her hair came off her head like ruffed up fleece, or a used Brillo pad, balling in blonde curls. When he approached her ("This may seem a bit forward, but..."), she simply smiled, took a sip from her wine, and listened to him blather on for several minutes about beauty and regret and how there were times when you had to take complete control of your life and not let yourself drift with the going tide. Didn't she agree? It was important to do things, right?

"Sometimes being forward is good."

Pause.

"I think maybe I should kiss you now..."

Her eyes were like an indeterminate pregnancy test, so pale blue they were nearly white.

But she was already moving past him, snatching the box of cigars from Miter's hands, clipping as many of the remaining offenders as she could about an inch past the cap. The tobacco spread open like torn pork. Eyes snapped open and closed like applause. Miter was a burnt ember. And Gage told Kitchen about working as a waitress for years in her hometown diner; serving quarter-sized cheeseburgers by the half-dozen to customers who barely acknowledged her, though they all knew her parents quite intimately; the smoke she could get out of her clothes but not her skin; the pain of swallowing; rushing to the back alley to puke; the other local teens giggling behind their joints; the confrontation with the balding chef who accused her of being "polemic;" the operation she needed but couldn't afford. "And it's not like people even came in there to eat or drink anyway, just to play those stupid video lottery machines. And we only served liquor in the first place cos the law told us we had to. We threw out the stale beer every six months like clockwork and nobody said boo, and the smoking just gave them something to do with the other hand. I tried to set up a collection system for cigarette butts. Did you know they can recycle the cellulose acetate into camera film and playing cards and Nike Air soles and filler for sleeping bags and, heck, we had a full garbage can of butts every week, and that's an entire sleeping bag right there! Trillions of cigarette butts are littered worldwide every year. Imagine how many sleeping bags we could get out of that..."

There was definitely something special about her, especially later, once they'd had a chance to get to know each other better, in the basement, where the countrified improv band was lined up along the concrete wall like shrapnel, with his hand up her skirt, his index and middle finger rolling like moistened newspaper. She tasted like a Madras curry. She was so still. Sighing and holding him tight.

"Excuse me, lovebirds..." Miter had somehow managed to extricate him ("But..."), was leading him back upstairs. The younger set had gathered around the music like flies, because it meant less effort at conversation, which Kitchen could admire at the moment. Miter pushed them aside, directed Kitchen into the washroom, shut the door. Kitchen stalked the toilet seat, seized it. Miter unzipped and approached the sink.

"Miter? Jesus!"

"Oh, don't tell me you've never done it."

"..."

"Whatever, dude." He reached out to run the hot water, and the tension in his shoulders fell off like shaves of cheese. "It's like the masturbation of the twenty-first century. Everyone admits to jerking off now and then, but just try to say you peed in someone's sink and they look at you like a monster. It's time we all took stock of our lives here, K, and lived up to the full potential of man. I pee in the sink. You pee in the sink. We all pee in the goddamn sink! And you know why?" Miter was barely looking at what he was doing. Kitchen's eyes were stuck on the stainless steel cup of toothbrushes. "Cos we can. It sets us apart from the apes or something. You laugh, but you think they have sinks?!" He zipped up, turned off the water, checked his hair in the mirror, finally looked Kitchen in the eye. "K, you don't want to date that one. Chick's got digestive problems."

"She doesn't have digestive problems. She's got a cyst on her esophagus."

"Sure it's not a callous?" He made lewd gestures.

"..."

"You know, dude, these things just work themselves out eventually...with friction."

Kitchen spent the next month in rapturous anticipation, imagining their future together, a stylized film full of wonderful product placements. There were so many things about her that he liked and admired. For one, she cared, about things, and was working toward one of those useless degrees that left you time for such... things. And since he'd already decided he didn't even have the inclination to think about those... things, well, Kitchen was glad she kept him apprised of what he *should* care about. The City was waging a war against the homeless. (He felt safer already.) Investigation by the Mexican National Institute of Ecology in the states of Oaxaca and Puebla had found bio-chemically contaminated maize varieties in fifteen of twenty-two communities tested, at levels from 3 to 10%. (The Mexicans stole Necedah's corn production too?!) Bush's plans to beef up his new Star Wars plan were jeopardizing the peace with Russia they'd been trying for so long to establish. And Dow Chemicals was feeding dibromo-chloropropane (DBCP) to poor people around the world, using them as chemical guinea pigs for whatever scheme—

"Wait a second, what was that last one?"

"Dow Chemicals? What they did in Bhopal alone as Union Carbide is enough to—"

"But Dow products have helped NASA boost every shuttle into space since the program started in 1981, I mean Dow Chemicals, wow, what if— did you— Dow Chemicals?! You think your dry cleaner's just blowing hot air on your Club Monaco blazer? Don't they even make CorningWare or something, or, wow, like, catgut sutures... silicone shunts... breast implants..."

She was glaring at him.

"They're all about living! Improved daily!"

"Everything comes at a price, Kitchen."

"Just try and give me a cheaper way to store food safely than GLAD bags..."

But he continued to meet her after work at the all-natural soap store ("But what do you *really* want to do with your life?" he asked her), and they discussed the woes of the world while screwing indiscriminately wherever they could find the time and space. Who knew there was so much going on out there? Did everyone think this way? How come it never showed up in their focus groups? Shouldn't there be a way to put a stop to it?

There was another protest downtown. An American spy plane had crash-landed in some Chinese paddy field, startling several illiterate farmers and ruining what had promised to be a real bumper rice crop. Since that was all they ate over there, people were understandably upset. The Chinese ambassador to Washington said the plane and its crew would be returned eventually, but first they wanted to make sure no national secrets had been revealed. Also, because the crash had occurred in such a remote area (it was a country built on remote areas), it would be near impossible to reach the crew for weeks, and even more difficult to get them out. The President had issued a strong warning to his Chinese counterpart, urging prudence and diplomacy. The families of those brave POWs set up a vigil in front of the Chinese embassy.

Of course, the plane had really crashed in Chongqing, a city of over thirty million people (making it one of the largest cities in the world). And the first people to reach the wreckage were the defensive line of Chongqing Tech's football squad, who'd been expecting another running play from Chongqing U but really weren't expecting to stop it, as they hadn't won a game against their cross-town rivals in twelve years. Yellow flags went up everywhere as Tech broke formation before the hike, several players brought out of their fierce concentration by the Doppler whine of the incoming EP-3, but CU quarterback Jiang Jiaxuan made a Marino-style fake to draw the remaining defense into a feigned sack, first handing off to all-star running back Qian "Pinball" Chen, who was nearly in the clear when the spy plane's emergency landing forced him out of bounds somewhere near the Tech twenty-three. Halted so early, the points showed up as a draw, and after a mad celebration unheard of in Chongqing Tech's history, the substitute centre, "Dragonball" Zhiang, was later cut from the team for passing out naked on the lawn of the university Chairman.

The American soldiers, stunned but uninjured, were all put up free of charge at the Harbour Plaza.

But the West still nurtured worries about "losing" to communism, and so it was important to portray the Yellow Dragon as a bunch of pointy-hatted slant-eyes with no shoes. The news channels ran old footage from the Vietnam War, sometimes even scenes from *M.A.S.H.* and *Apocalypse Now*. CNN explained how the reconnaissance aircraft—it was decided that "spy plane" had seriously faulty connotations—probably didn't even exist any more, picked over by the scavenging Chinese poor. If it was discovered that they played football like other normal North American youths...

Well...

Swan was the first to update them on the anti-protest:

"So this group of Chinese Buddhists have placed themselves between the families of the soldiers and the embassy, right, and the families are looking at this like it's some kind of hostile move. But get this: because they're Buddhists, the Chinese are basically just ignoring them, standing around practicing their Feng Shui and all. Everyone figures it's going to blow up pretty soon—"

"Feng Shui? What are they doing, rearranging the potted plants outside to line up better with the aura of the candles?"

"Jesus, Miter, I don't know anything about this slowed down kung fu shit, do I look like some kind of Ginsu master?"

Kitchen couldn't take his eyes off the television. Even at home, when the choices seemed almost limitless these days, he was soothed by the flippant rhetoric of the US Defense Secretary, coaxed into false understanding by the Press Secretary. How could a society survive without advertising? What did they talk about on their way to work, or on the assembly lines, where the reporters claimed they performed their tasks without complaint ("That's bullshit," Roast threw a sponge brick at the screen. "How can things get better if we don't complain?"), or when they drove home in their nameless, government-issue automobiles, with nothing to look at but buildings and people. And the rice paddies, of course. ("Shit, look, there's another one... Are those American soldiers carrying surfboards?") The place was full of them. Government-issue houses with government-issue families where they sent their government-issue magazines; anorexic magazines starved of their tear-away subscription cards and peel-away perfume samples, their send-away back section and look-away nudie shots; stunted magazines with nothing but stringy government-issue content. Did the Chinese eat at McDonald's? Could they recite the Big Mac song? Did they communicate in glib slogans and catchphrases like the rest of the world? Or were their TVs filled with endless propaganda, shots of the Chairman sitting in front of his own TV, watching TV just like them, one exactly the same size as their TVs, eating fried rice and sweet and sour chicken balls, chop suey, everything equal and regulated. Did they have TVs?

The nation was united, but surprised. Hadn't they won the war against communism years ago? Wasn't that the reason they'd persecuted their own entertainment industry? Otherwise, what was the point? Now, here they were in the twenty-first century, doing the whole thing all over again. And what was it that separated them from the communists? TVs. Even Gage could sit in front of the TV all day, not really doing anything exactly, just sitting, with the television on but the sound turned off.

"I don't know, I guess I like the visual stimulation, I'm not actually watching it."

"But how can you take your eyes away from it?"

Shrug.

He grabbed for the remote. "But listen, this spot doesn't really work without sound, I mean, otherwise those frogs are just croaking away like... well, like nothing, and—"

"Is that all that really concerns you, Kitchen, I mean, TV's alright and all, but it's not just a tool for salesmen to peddle their crappy ab-toners and fat free grills—"

"Of course it is... but it's more than that... more than ab-toners and pharmaceuticals and even psychic hotlines, it's a medium to sell anything you want. You think television is— god, how do I put this? What do you think was the purpose of the first television set?"

"Oh, who cares, Kitchen, broadcast the Berlin Olympics, maybe?"

"Bullshit. Why would we need to see things we'd never seen before? The purpose of the first TV was simply to sell TVs."

End of story.

He'd decided that selling himself had everything as much to do with the media buy as it did with the pitch itself. It was important that Gage not see him too much, lest she grow tired or annoyed. Pressured. At the same time, he wanted her to remember his brand, to favour it, to reach for it. Thankfully, they were so new to each other, so full of stories that hadn't yet grown boring. He told her about the time he met the Pope ("I was wearing that thing as a necklace for days before somebody explained what it was…"). And she told him about the time she'd come home drunk at three in the morning, barely fifteen, puking in the toilet while her mother held back her hair, imploring her sister—seated on the edge of the bathtub—not to tell. He hadn't had sex until he was eighteen, on that same trip to Europe, with some gap-toothed girl from Ohio, and when his friend came back to the hotel room before they were even naked, refusing to leave, they went into the bathroom to finish, running all the faucets on full as she went down on him on the edge of the bidet. When Gage was thirteen, growing up in rural Canada, she'd tried to keep her breathing low, masturbating to episodes of *Neon Rider* in the kitchen while her father watched *Hockey Night in Canada* in the den.

"Oh, Dr. Michael Terry, I've been delinquent, let's go riding…"

At the same time, he did everything he could to hide the differences he perceived between them, tried to focus only on the advantages. Not even her idiosyncratic tendencies seemed to bother him. The age difference. The gum chewing. The cats.

"Tell me," Kitchen was picking the stray hairs off the sleeve of his jacket while seated on her couch. "How come so many vegetarians have cats, I mean, why is it okay for your pets to eat meat when you find it so abhorrent?"

But she wasn't one of the impulsive followers who made so little sense to him. She had a logical answer for everything. She was an intellectual environmentalist, a meritocratic vegetarian, which meant she only ate animals that were particularly dumb, like turkeys and fish. For the most part, she ate nothing but cheese on bagels, anyway, possibly with capers or horseradish, and was afraid of fresh tomatoes and green pepper, wouldn't touch any food that had come in contact with them, all of which dramatically reduced any possibility of finding anything to make for dinner.

For her part, Gage was attracted to Kitchen's innocence. She'd been at Swan's party for hours before they met, before anyone was ready to start flirting. They were all concerned they might peak before they were ready to head home. So they ate M&Ms and Cheetos in near silence. They spoke in low volume and pretended they didn't need alcohol to be interested in each other. A small group in the hallway had invented a game called Rock Paper Anything, and had attracted a small uncommunicative group as they exposed their palsied fists in representation of venetian blinds, a bag of marbles, a bishop. One, two, three:

"Umbrella."

"Cactus."

"Umbrella keeps sun off cactus, cactus dies."

One, two, three:

"Asteroid colliding with Earth."

"Crash test dummy."

"Crash test dummy feels no pain, crash test dummy wins."

One, two, three:

"Pancreas."

"Bottle of vermouth."

"A tie!"

Kitchen, however, arrived late, carefully avoiding any conversation by studying the workmanship of the home, admiring the cabinetry, running a finger along the bevelled moulding. He commented occasionally on the south-facing exposure ("So many people go for esthetics before efficiency these days. In the old days, they knew..."), the exposed ceiling beams ("I'm intrigued by the sporadic placement of the load..."), and the open-concept kitchen ("The most important ingredient in any dish should be conversation..."). He was charming and introspective, obsessed with any and all abstract concepts, so long as they didn't involve any reaction or empathy on his part, like physics ("So, maybe the speed of light is actually zero..."), the premonitions of early science fiction ("You know there's a guy who actually claims to have predicted anti-gravity sex? As if the astronauts are already rutting around up there like middle-aged singles?"), the conflict of the urban and the rural. Fame was a particular favourite. The Russians, he tried to tell Gage, had sent *several* dogs into space over the years. Not just the famous Laika they abandoned, no, in 1960, Belka and Strelka both returned from separate "orbits" of fifty and seventy kilometres respectively. What was it about this one mutt that had everyone dreaming of some other world beyond, inspiring songwriters like Bowie, filmmakers like Kubrick, deifying this mongrel because she was a pawn of Fate, when all she probably did was shit all over the entire capsule with no land in sight, and no human to tell her different? No master to stop her from ripping out the seat cushions, destroying part of them, eating most of them, throwing up in the corner. No, no corners! A perfectly round capsule! Sterile as a virgin's underwear. Too stupid to think of biting her handlers and making a break for it. "For this, we all know the name of Laika the cosmomutt?"

"What are you talking about?"

"Lord knows..."

She had no idea he worked in advertising. Just that he had a mouth like a beatifically infected scar, lips swollen around the thin-rimmed crack of his toothless smile, and eyes like sweating plastic, blue as sorrow. He was in possession of a skillful dismissal of others' opinions. He talked about existing outside morality. Through Chaos Theory, he claimed, any and all actions could be seen to effect the entire world in some way. Only when issues were narrowed down to the specific could one make the distinction between what was good or not good for that individual. "You give your leftover squash-stuffed cannelloni in cream sauce to some disadvantaged, forty-year-old runaway sleeping in his box over a subway grate. You feel good. He's got fine cuisine in his belly for once. But giving food to one homeless beggar is, essentially, preventing the next poor trash picker down the street from eating it. Plus, your rich meal probably gives the bugger cramps and the runs for weeks, and only prolongs the inevitable moment when the blood in his veins finally freezes solid, when you're walking by some other night and think he's asleep underneath that half sleeping bag.

"It's a more selective genocide, as opposed to total indifference, which is much more passive and humane."

He was drunk, not quite focussing on any of them as he moved to the centre of the living room, pointing fingers, drawing stares. But Gage drew him aside.

"What do you think happens to those people, like, the homeless ones who die like that? I mean, just burying someone costs over two thousand dollars. And that's not even including the box or the gravestone or even the funeral—"

"Who would go?"

"What do you mean 'who would go'? The question is who *can* go? Cos there won't be a funeral, you know? They can barely afford to eat, how do you think they can blow the average nine thousand on dying?"

"There should be a way," he offered.

"Yes, there should," she agreed.

Gage didn't move in with him because they were in love. Those sorts of things came to her much more slowly. But he wasn't really looking for signs of rejection. And she was too addicted to the attention to tell him. She also had nowhere else to go and he had this whole empty house he bought with his new raise, god, what else was he going to do with all that room otherwise? She'd lost her job at the soap store (i.e., Pure) because she refused to follow their new sales policy, a marketing strategy carefully designed to build on the Pure brand name, so that people went home remembering their name and not just "the soap store." She found the whole thing repulsive, especially for a company that claimed to be so caring and good for you. "I don't know what they're all about, you know, but it's just not what *I'm* about, you follow me? I mean holy— I'm in this retail business to help people, what's all this, 'Have you ever been to Pure before?' Who cares? Are we supposed to offer the repeat customers worse treatment because we've already got them hooked? Or do they get to move to the front of the line because they give us more money? Crooked shits... Just cos they open up a few more stores they forget the ideals they started with? Well, they can go ahead and fire me, you hear me?! Assholes! Cos I for one will not become one of your global conquest pawns!"

Gage spent the next week marching out front with a sign that said PURE SOAPS ARE PEOPLE, which of course nobody got because that movie was so freaking obscure, Kitchen told her, couldn't she pick something a little more culturally relevant? And besides, the word "pure" just made the whole thing confusing, at least she could have painted it using the store logo or something...

Kitchen's new house was in the latest trendy part of town, in what was soon to become the un-hip area once again. The used appliance stores and ethnic take-outs were making way for renovated condo spaces. But there were still plenty of prostitutes and abandoned gas stations, pushers on every second corner, people who peed themselves and didn't care. The reverse psychology of real estate. Whereas the earlier generation had cramps whenever they even thought about this district, it had become all the rage to retire as early as possible, working like mad until you'd wasted your youth entirely. Cutting corners (i.e. "slumming it," not having children) had replaced excess, at least when it came to real estate.

Kitchen's home had been neglected for so long, however, even the appliances he got with the place were disgusting. He'd used a can of Easy-Off on the stove, but he'd done such a poor job wiping it clean that there were still white powdery marks on every side like dried toothpaste. There was a strange odour every time he turned it on. He was sure he was slowly poisoning himself to death.

Gage suggested he clean it again, but where was the time?

Likewise, the sewer flap on the home's plumbing had malfunctioned somehow, refused to shut. And the odour of human waste came from the drain whenever the water was run, making Kitchen gag uncontrollably when he was brushing his teeth. Thinking maybe it was just a hair clog ("Do you have to cut your hair directly over the sink?"), he used bottle after bottle of Drano until the fumes from the chemicals at least masked the stench.

"And that's better?" Gage confronted him, her eyes red and accusing.

"At least I know that stuff's sterile."

Plus, it was an easier solution than hiring a plumber to rip the walls apart. Certainly cheaper. Drano had recently become a client. He just brought another sample home every night.

"Think of it as deodorant for the sewer... shit, that's gold, where did I put my pen?"

Drano's main problem was its image. For some reason, there had been a rash of dogs dying lately from licking the empty containers, and several animal rights groups had taken it up as a cause. Miter tried to argue that everything ("Including chocolate, I mean, hey—this is chocolate, people!") was toxic to dogs, and that dogs were by no means the smartest of god's creatures so we really shouldn't feel so bad about it. But it was hard to counter PETA's "I'd rather wear nothing at all than poison my dog" demonstration. Or the billboard campaign sponsored by the SPCA: *Man's best friend's worst enemy*.

"Have they seen what this stuff can do to a nasty clog?" Roast was up on the boardroom table again. "This stuff should *replace* the dog as man's best friend! Nude supermodels, geez, how do you fight that shit..."

When both Drano and Liquid-Plumr started losing ground to the more enviro-friendly alternatives on the market, they needed another angle, some way to defeat this obvious attack on "relatively hazard-free" chemicals. Miter devised several visual interpretations for Kitchen's deodorant angle. A bottle of Drano with a roll top. A spray bottle. A bottle with a plug on the back inserted into the wall outlet. For a while they even toyed with the possibility of using it as a weed-killer ("Grass *smass*, will it kill the weeds or not?"). But in the end, instead of butting heads with the likes of Power Plumber and equally successful home remedies (two handfuls of baking soda with half a cup of vinegar achieved the same results), they took their chemical formula to the family planning market instead. Brilliant! Just urinate in a glass container and then add Crystal Drano. If it turns green you're having a girl, blue-black it's a boy. Cheaper than an ultrasound (approx. $200) by far. Especially since you didn't use the entire canister in one go. A complete family planning kit for only $2.69, no matter how many children you plan to have.

The only problems were legal ones, solved by a simple **Warning: Fumes may induce vomiting and/or esophageal**

burns. Keep away from eyes. Do not urinate directly into beaker containing Crystal Drano. If possible, perform test outside.

Unfortunately, no one wanted to pee outside. And sales dropped dramatically. Because of its new relationship to babies, consumers figured it wasn't strong enough to unclog drains any more.

They scrapped the entire campaign.

Miter's Inactivist Group was growing larger in the office every day. Like Kool-Aid soaking into a Bounty paper towel. Not that he invited it, mind you. He'd already learned that lesson. It was simply the perfect environment for it. They were all so engrossed in their own lives, they had no time for anything external. Miter had gone around to every television in the agency putting parental blocks on all the news stations. The kid who delivered their papers was instructed to leave nothing but the Arts and Reviews sections. Group meetings were never announced, were held only by chance when they passed each other in the hallway, silent nods sliding by on grunts of indifference.

As the other creatives realized Miter wasn't actually doing anything ("My computer's doing funny things, I'm going home."), they put down their pens in protest. Fair was fair, after all. No one skipped lunch. No one stayed past five. And when they *were* there, they stared across the dividers daring each other to do work, the threat of unemployment hanging over them like an ominous wave of Ocean Spray.

What's the matter? Getting a little nervous? Want to work, maybe?

Nope. Could sit here doing nothing all day. You?

No worries at all…

No one noticed.

They existed in a one-floor utopian society without global worry or strife.

Gage, however, was having an even greater effect on Kitchen.

"Isn't it important to make a difference?"

"What difference? K, what's this girl done to you?"

It was beginning to look like Gage was the only thing grounding him these days. It was too bad they seemed to be drifting apart. The homeless she kept talking about, for example, were something completely outside Kitchen's frame of reference, people who neither sold nor purchased anything. People who were untouched by great creative concepts. What could you do with the homeless when they died? Sure as heck, he didn't know. But Gage was the one who could make him see the worth in all this. Around her he felt energized. Good. And he listened with something akin to interest as she laid out her plan to introduce public burial plots, purchased by the City, that could even double as additional green space with a battery of wind-harvesters and an urban bird sanctuary and—wow!

He checked his watch.

"Hey, if we hurry, we might be able to catch that premiere tonite. They're premiering the new Opel spot before the film, for a launch over here, I hear the Vivaro is really going to revolutionize the American cargo van market..."

"What is it that you want, Kitchen? I think you have to decide that before we can really go any further, you know, cos like I'm sitting here with all these goals and ideals and shit and you're bringing so little to the table. I mean, you're very talented, man, find some way to support the arts or something. Volunteer with the opera company, or the national ballet... Or get a job with one of the environmental groups..."

He wanted to impress her, have her look at him with shining belief. Or at least something akin to belief. Respect, maybe? Or at least curiosity?

He wanted to share things with her.

"You make me feel like maybe there *is* something to believe in, you know? Like maybe all I have to do is find it, and everything will suddenly become apparent. Right? So maybe if I could write some spots for these friends of yours. At least help *them* get heard. Get them some corporate sponsorship—"

"O, god, Kitchen, you just don't get it, maybe this... this dating thing... isn't such a good idea."

"Dating isn't an idea, honey, it's more like an instinct of preservation..."

"It's just that we're such different people—"

"No, wait, I gotta write that one down for later, I think maybe I can use it in this spot for RRSPs—"

"—and we really have so little in common, god, I mean you have this platform and it seems like you could really make a difference and— this is just ridiculous..."

"No, no, wait, Gage, don't hang up, I'm just kidding..."

For a second, the dial tone sounded like she was thinking about it.

Shortly before they split, Kitchen arranged for her to come out to the Tagline. A relationship was all about hard work. Surely their two worlds would fit together if forced hard enough. But the others didn't understand her. She thought crop marks were found in farmers' fields, and that a double truck was some kind of slang for a pickup with extra support wheels. She admired the beauty in some television spots, but couldn't remember the product when hard-pressed. Couldn't care less, really (if you really wanted to get down to it). In fact (and she found this difficult to express to Kitchen because he still seemed so sweet and innocent to her, so she drank even more), she thought of advertising as a lesser evil, but an evil all the same. Kitchen, who never once asked her about these feelings, found himself continually covering for her ("No, you mean Toyota, don't you, honey?"), but he could see the looks the others gave her.

Plus, in this environment, he noticed she didn't move right, was a sandal girl, hadn't grown into the heels that were so popular these days, the ones all the other girls were wearing. They thrust her upper body forward like a KFC chicken, so top-heavy she could barely stumble to the little girls' room after her fifth drink. "Phew, man, sometimes this stuff just runs through me," she winked when she toddled back into the booth. "You know what I mean? Sometimes I wish I *had* a clog down there somewhere. So I could carry on a normal conversation for once, where two people say things back and forth for more than a half-hour? You know, man, I've never been to this place before it's, I don't know, it makes you feel like you're in New York or something, all that dark wood and those guys wearing suits." Sip. "Only they're not wearing suits, right? Just look at them! Not a suit in the bunch. But they all walk around like they're in suits, like they're always taking off ties that aren't there, patting their breast pockets for wallets or hankies and like, hey, somehow all stuffy and businesslike but trying so hard not to be... Isn't that weird?" Sip, sip. "Not that I'm complaining, really, I kind of like it. It's like a zoo, where the world doesn't even exist for them outside this habitat. Could sit and watch them all day..."

Kitchen tried to show her how similar they were to her. These people were upset about things, too. Things that *mattered*. Like homelessness. Or sweat shops. The skyrocketing price of professional sporting events, with its direct corollary to players' salaries. Even the shortcomings of public transport:

"You want me to ride it to work every day? It stinks!"

"Maybe it wouldn't be so bad if we could just clear the bums out of it. This old fucker pissed himself on the train the other day. Basically got a whole car to himself and no one else could find a place to sit."

"You, sir, are a model of compassion."

"Liberal..."

"Maybe we just pay the homeless to play hockey? I'm sure they'd do it for minimum wage. Solve two problems at once."

And the Oscars had, once again, been a travesty.

"I had a dream about him last night." This from Gage, on the subject of Best Director. She thought maybe this was a good opportunity to bond with Kitchen's friends, outside of irony, sarcasm, or any subject that mattered to her.

"Will there be any nudity in this dream? I need another drink and don't want to miss anything good."

"I was visiting my friend in New York— you met her, Kitchen— the one with the pierced tongue..."

"Mmmmm...."

"Have you two ever... you know...?"

"And in the dream we went to see the launch of this guy's new movie and a party afterward. I thought it looked like ass, but everyone kept telling him he was a genius, and I mean, it was so obvious they were all total idiots..."

"Please tell me you went down on him then."

Sex. Their lives revolved around it. They pawed at each other beneath tabletops, leaned in close and grazed on ears and necks. Even the homely swapped obvious gropes by the bar, licked hungrily at unshaven faces, cupped flesh they hoped were breasts. Gage was like a new toy to them. And she was so serious, so much more intellectual. She liked to read, or at least the illusion of reading. She lit up over Virginia Woolf, had lost friends over Ayn Rand. She'd picked up a copy of Neil Bauer's *Tower* through Amazon, and made sure to hold it on her lap while riding the subway, left it lying on the floor beside the StairMaster, even lined it up with the edge of the table when they switched booths to get away from his friends. "The reviews are amazing, listen to this... Ready? Just stop looking around at everyone else for a second and look, okay, good... So this one guy says, are you listening, he says this is 'the future of fiction,' and he's not the only one, see, right here? There's pages of this stuff. Must mean something. I mean, some people might say he just wrote a bunch of unrelated lists, but there's something really powerful, I think, in words without grammar. It's like a message of *being*. Not *doing* anything at all, you know, but like, just there..."

But what kind of sense did that make? Sounded like this guy Bauer was a real nutcase and he was turning the whole world into a bunch of crackers. Words were for communicating, preferably the benefits of the latest vacuum or car model. Gimmicky bastard, everyone spent so much time reading ads these days, the poets and novelists had to come up with something crazy just to get noticed. Meanwhile they were losing sight of the whole narrative point.

"You just don't get it," she said.

"Don't get what?"

"Sometimes there are people who think different from you, you know? Speak different, want different, it's like you don't even speak the same language? And you, well, hey, I'm not saying anything but— Have you ever considered for once that things aren't the way they should be?"

"..."

"..."

"Oh— you're serious?"

"Kitchen, I'm going home now."

Kitchen admired the crowd mentality as it swayed and coalesced. He'd fallen over in the washroom unzipping his pants to piss, and he'd hit his head against the urinal. Everyone was looking at him funny. Had the band stopped? No, impossible. They were just between songs. All the televisions had been turned off. Someone Kitchen didn't know slipped him a blank business card. He waited until the band had lurched into their next tune before helping himself to their pitcher and escaping back into the crowd.

Someone was yelling at him. He felt like a brilliant star. Alone and dense.

He'd lost his peripheral vision, was walking into people without apology, hunting for the bar, turning his head slowly from side to side because he couldn't find it. Someone offered him some pills and he took them without asking what they were. He was certain, for a moment, that he was dancing, or at least that his hand was on someone's waist, but when he blinked, she was gone. And he wasn't even on the dance floor, just leaning up against the wall, which was hardly what he had intended in the first place ("Excuse me…"), finally spotting the bar again ("Sorry…"), heaving himself in that direction.

"Hey guy, are you okay? I mean, you don't look so hot… Yo, waiter-guy! Can I have one of those rags?" And someone was wiping his forehead with something that smelled vaguely of mold. Possibly even some Drano. It came away dark and heroic, and she squeezed the excess water into a glass on the bar.

"There has to be more than this…" Kitchen was barely coherent. He felt neatly triumphant.

"Sure there is, baby."

"I mean, how can we be expected to be satisfied with this shit when it doesn't continue to improve? You know? When you hit your peak somewhere around six and the rest of your life feels like some kind of unrealized potential?" Her hand was on his knee. When he closed his eyes, he could imagine she was someone else. "Maybe the only way to feel different is to make a difference? Right?" Hmm… "Are you going to drink that?" It tasted like that pale, delicious rag. Metallic. "I think maybe doing the right thing makes you feel right. Do you ever see those protesters agonizing over what to do with their lives? Shit, no, cos they're making the world a better place. Like water running downhill, you know? Doing what they're supposed to do… I think that might be it… I think that might be the answer."

"I think maybe you should come home with me tonight."

"What a strange thought…"

She leaned in too close, began stroking the back of his neck. "You know," she whispered. "I have a three-inch clit."

"Lady," he squeezed the bar. "You're a guy."

The air was full of so much disappointment.

part iii. winter.

The job cancellations continued straight through the third quarter. The fourth was barely beginning and already Kitchen's client wanted to hold off payment until the spring. There were profit expectations to meet. They weren't seeing any results from the ads they *were* making. Plus, there was additional civil unrest. And not just in their third world production facilities, either, no, right here at home, among the sales staff, the maintenance crews, the monitoring teams in Dallas. Internally, they'd put a stop to all air travel, using the impending threat of terrorism as a justifiable excuse. But did they expect people to buy that? With increased airport security, it was probably the safest time to wing it in the history of flight. Was it likely that terrorists would really hijack planes out of Wisconsin? And what indication had they ever given that they actually cared about the welfare of their employees? Was this, at last, the un-sellable concept? Roast tried to put up a strong front ("Capitalism was built on credit, Kitchen. If we cut them off now, where will we find the jobs of tomorrow?"), but it was clear to everyone on both sides of the agency walls that something was not right.

"Good." Miter was playing with a design in Photoshop, placing little Hitler moustaches on the models in the far background, adding extra fingers, removing legs in larger crowd scenes, anything to make the image inexplicably off. "That's the way it should be. The cogs keep moving but they're not connected to each other in any way. Perfectly smooth. No teeth..."

But what about progress?

"That's what I want my advertising signature to be, K." The pile of briefs on Miter's desk was growing more unmanageable with each day. "Extra fingers."

What about making the world a better place?

"For fuck's sake, I thought you broke up with that girl…"

But, Kitchen was still trying to think of some way he could win her (i.e., Gage) back, deciding that his main fault in this whole thing was simply customer service. He'd never really understood all that stuff about conservation and sustainability, but he should have realized it was important to her and at least pretended. He came home from work one day to find the front door unlocked, the extra set of keys on top of his humidor, and all those bottles of Drano with their lids permanently glued shut. Gone back to live with some of her hippie friends. Eight or nine of them in a three-bedroom semi-detached with only one or two jobs between them. She left him a note. She'd been tempted by Kitchen's standard of living, but now wanted free of his flagrant consumerism. At least for a while. She'd taken all the peanut butter and toilet paper.

Now that she was gone, Kitchen found he couldn't do without her. Being alone was not only emotionally draining, it was also time-consuming. The constant proximity to potentiality. Every woman he saw on the street was a potential sale. Every bit of conversation that didn't turn into a phone number was a failure. He was constantly having to decide if girls at work were hitting on him, or thought he was hitting on them, or were worth hitting on.

He had to think. Why would she ever take him back? What new services did he have to offer her?

He needed to see her. He needed to talk to her.

There were things she had at her place that belonged to him.

All Kitchen wanted was to understand one person. He didn't even expect anyone to understand him back. He was too complex. But getting into the head of one other person didn't seem so hard. He did it every day at work, albeit on a more collective basis.

For a while he thought he'd found that in Trapeza. She was so delightfully predictable, with her casual objectivity ("Is that what this is? Love?") and stoic remove ("Go fuck yourself, then, see if I care!"); her stylish yet sensible wardrobe. She spoke in such consistent journalistic cadences, with puns like shields, every word shouldering the import of steel-eyed practicality. Even in sex, faster, harder, roll me over, stick your tongue in my ass, she was like an instructional manual on audio tape. It was only in the end that he realized he hardly knew her at all.

Not even Miter made any sense to him, so obsessed had he become with the whole Inactivist thing. Deciding finally to have no beliefs at all, he suddenly resented those of others. When the Pope visited the City for World Youth Day, the streets were overrun with horny little teenage Christians. Miter drove around with a "*Honk if you love Jesus!*" bumper sticker, giving the finger to anyone who so much as waved at him.

At first Miter kept things on a fairly personal level. He flagged down taxis and refused to announce a proper destination. He'd taken to wearing his bathrobe and slippers to work. And he'd begun advocating resistance towards taxes. Hell, what could be better? No papers to fill out. No undue stress. If the government didn't have their money, how could it continue to function? How could it fund the programs in which he had no personal stake?

Perfect.

The only problem was that no one else seemed behind him.

"Are you crazy? No one's done anything around here for weeks."

"These people? Do you think they count? Look at them, K, it's like a zoo full of monkeys! Except they don't even chew gum or play with themselves, they're so boring."

The Agency had been, as an experiment, a fine example of Miter's theoretical Inactivist society. At least it proved a few things. Without the media, the world as they knew it would begin to break down. One month after establishing his news embargo, not one person could correctly identify a hit song from the radio, let alone the current politicians. No one could comment on the debate—spearheaded by the new governor of Wisconsin—to re-legalize corn. Once Miter took away their access to the rest of the world, they seemed to gravitate towards a centre of complete and utter disengagement, the mindless protectors of the status quo. Without clear cut examples from which to draw guidance, they didn't even talk to one another, they were so unclear on how regular human beings were supposed to behave. They were wild beasts to each other.

The sight of so much blatant self-satisfaction only began to sicken him. "It's like a game for them, like they've decided to have some sort of theme day around here, wear prom dresses, grow neck beards, I don't know, they just don't get it. I mean, look at Swan. Would you fucking look at Swan! Give them an excuse to take their clothes off and— Swan, no one wants to see that— Geez-zus!"

"I thought you were just sick of people asking you to donate money."

"Dude, if we just do nothing, what's to separate us from the people who are just plain lazy? You know? We're not a bunch of fat old men sitting on the couch all day watching golf and picking our asses. We're not unaware. We just don't care!"

"OK, but what about the—"

"Kitchen, man, you're the copywriter, start getting this shit down."

There were a few staff keeping the Agency afloat during all this. Roast, mostly. But others as well. Miter chewed out a Junior Account Coordinator ("What the fuck are you talking about?"), simply because he asked him to work at all ("It takes you four days to write the goddamn brief and you need three concepts in two days?"), and Miter sent the poor thing back to his side of the building ("Fuck!"), where he hid in one of the abandoned offices until the tears stopped coming ("Why don't you learn to do your job instead of bothering me with this shit?!"). When Roast drifted in like the smell of burning pastry, Miter launched his keyboard against the wall.

"How can they expect to work with this ridiculous thing? See how small it is? What is it with Macintosh and their miniscule keyboards? Ah! Ah! My fingers can't even hit one key at a— look, my god, they're huge. These hands! Hideous! I must be one hideous beast of a man."

"Don't get started, Miter— listen— stop moving around, you idiot, I suppose it's the economy of design, is that what you—"

"And the IBM clones are the evil SUVs of the keyboard industry? I'm supposed to feel guilty for wanting a little more luxury around here? They're a perfectly reasonable size, Roast. You know it, and I know it."

"..."

"So help me, god, get me a normal keyboard in here so I can get some goddamn work done!"

A week later, Miter stopped coming in to work altogether. As he told Kitchen, Inactivism wasn't just something you could get on and off like a bus, you had to live it. Twenty-four/seven. And if he wanted the movement to spread, to effect people outside of his direct sphere of influence, he needed to be more committed. Within a year, he guaranteed, the streets would be safe from canvassers.

No one, no matter where they lived or what side they stood for, would be able to invoke any sort of change again. They wouldn't even want it. They would stop caring about the way everyone else lived, the geo-political world subdivided into tiny little parties of one.

"It's about rights, Kitchen. And the primary right in any free political system should be the right to keep everyone else from taking part!"

The political landscape in America was changing. The people had grown disillusioned with the flesh and the blood. So many candidates cut from the same cloth. The paper dolls of policy. Spouting the same boisterous tripe about jobs and tax cuts and health care and public execution. The denial of affairs. The people wanted something more.

Something more unique.

The answer came, as usual, from television. But with the exhaustion of celebrity as a polling draw (Reagan gave way to Sonny Bono who gave way to Jesse "The Body" Ventura, and then where else could they go?), both parties turned to the heroes of the hard sell. And why not? They were so lovable and impish, approachable and focussed. Of course, Lucky the Leprechaun was ineligible because he was born on foreign soil. And Toucan Sam's famous nose was judged to be too Jewish to take the South. But for a short while, Tony the Tiger seemed sure of a nod from the Republican side; he was in good shape but not too young, able to jog with the press but not without lines on his face. It was only in the end that they decided there might be too much public confusion with his Exxon counterpart. And with the nation in its present state, all eyes turned to Cap'n Crunch. His military background was just what the country needed to pull through this trying episode in history.

The Democrats, not to be left behind, responded with Aunt Jemima, the first black woman to ever run on the ticket.

Of course, entering the political arena was only an excuse to bring out the big guns. They'd been polite with each other for so long, these forces of economics, unwilling to sink as low as they needed to win. Under this new guise of political messaging, companies enjoyed the freedom to drag each other through the muck, most of the claims untrue. And PepsiCo took one last shot at 7UP, trying to knock it from the peak of the carbonated lemon sodas (a feat where they were unsuccessful with Slice). With a campaign centred around the uncola's dubious past, when the secret recipe included (among other things) a healthy dose of lithium (*Takes the ouch out of grouch*), known to induce diarrhea and acne, not to mention thyroid and kidney problems.

...which sent Kitchen back to his sick bed.

Had he ingested any of it (i.e., 7UP) in the past thirty years? It was unavoidable, he supposed, what with summers by the pool, the cub scout campouts, the school field trips. He'd grown up in such a misunderstood democracy, where grownups decided an even split of choice was somehow better for the world, rather than letting the kids decide for themselves. Who could blame them, really? When they were young, choice had been so limited, and the drink of choice was always alcohol. Now, the children fought for pole position at the cooler, and baptized their tiny fists in the icy redeemer, their Cokes or Pepsis born high over their oversized heads. When the 7UP was all that was left, you didn't care because deep down it was really just the sugar you were after, anyway.

At any rate, Kitchen could safely assume to have drunk, in a moderate estimate, a couple hundred accidental 7UPs. The big question: was it enough to have upset the delicate balance of his body? One day Kitchen noticed a hard bump on his neck directly below his right ear. He thought at first it might be a pimple, but it was harder and seemed more independent from his skin, a tiny bit of calcified growth, something he could push around with his finger like a bubble inside a vacuumed seal. A blocked artery? Or a vein? Maybe that was the reason he'd had such trouble getting that erection. He spent most of the day online, surfing every free diagnosis site he could find, marvelling at the banner ads for 24-hour heartburn relief, Viagra, Atkins diet products ("What is that? Online bacon?"), and finally he realized he was dying. *Sore neck, cough, hoarseness, hard bumps*, he had all those things. No wonder he'd been feeling so down, playing video games all day, eating nothing but toast.

Thyroid cancer.

All because of the little bit of lithium in an innocent childhood sugar fix.

Gage wasn't returning his phone calls.

He called Trapeza.

"I know what you're thinking, that cancer isn't something that normally hits people my age, but the web site says it's pretty common in people twenty to thirty-nine. Or at least you should get it checked out every two years during that period, which seems like an awful lot to me, doesn't it?"

"You should have them check for ovarian cancer, too."

"Well, fuck, Trap, it's only that I might be dying and all, and I thought maybe you'd like to patch up any loose ends or—"

"Kitchen, you're not dying, every time you get a bloody nose you think you're going to hemorrhage past the point of no return. Have you ever thought of seeing someone about your head?"

"That's what I'm trying to tell you, Trap, it's right on my goddamn neck—"

"First of all, there are no loose ends. Is that clear? And secondly, remember the time you had that dizzy spell on the highway and the shock from it made you think you'd had a heart attack? Twenty-eight years old and the first thing that comes to your mind is that you'd had a heart attack."

"God, my whole left side was tingling, and I couldn't even speak, *ah... dough... no... wha... happe, hep... me*, doesn't that sound like a stroke now? Doesn't it? Plus, my grandfather—"

"—was nearly twice the age you were, can we— Kitchen, shut up— look, can we just stop talking about this for a second and— That's it, I'm hanging up..."

"No, wait, Trap I don't know who else to turn to and— shit, can you hold on a second, there's someone, I— Jesus, Swan can't you see I'm on the phone, can't this wait? Alright? Okay, Trap, I'm back, but I needed to tell you about—"

"Kitchen, I have work to do."

"No, shut up for a second, this is important..."

"You still know how to sweet talk'm."

"...wait, listen: 'Trouble swallowing. Breathing problems like feeling as if one were breathing through a straw'..."

"Ever heard of a cold, Kitchen? Take a Sudafed or something—"

"Can we be serious for a second here, I mean, Gage says there are chemicals in the air all the time, you know, from industry and shit, and these things can cause everything from emphysema to Tourette's Syndrome and god knows what else. Thankfully most American companies these days are using more friendly toxins, I know, I just wrote some of those spots, seems these sulfates can actually give people superhuman powers in some cases, but I grew up in all that smog and filth, who knows what kind of irreparable damage—"

"Who's Gage? "

"This girl I'm seeing, doesn't matter, she says—"

"Is this why you called me? To tell me about your new girlfriend? Why can't you tell *her* about your neck acne and let me get some work done, I've got a story that needs to be vetted and produced by the six o'clock and if I don't finish it I'll be standing there talking about my new suit for four minutes—"

"Gage? I don't know, she's into all these alternative healing things, and I've tried to be open-minded about it all, you know, Trap, but— well, it's all so untested in a fair and open market, there's never really been much advertising except maybe in the back of comic books, and that hardly counts... We're planning to work on something together, I think, maybe I can help out some of her causes, you know? Turn my talents to good, as she says..."

"Fuck you."

"At least my friends *like* her!"

He got his break (i.e., Burningham Barnum) as a copywriter in the late fifties. Barnum might not have been completely responsible for Doyle Dane Bernbach's "Think small" Volkswagen campaign of that period. In fact, he worked on almost none of the print, radio or television spots. But he was still the real brains behind the tiny German car's early success in North America, practically inventing spectacle—or stunt—advertising. While Julian Koenig and Helmut Krone were turning traditional advertising on its ear with their self-deprecating copy and vast sheets of unused white, Barnum introduced the world to the Punchbuggy. Hiring several dozen youthful-looking midgets in the influential suburbs and burrows of Los Angeles, New York City and San Francisco ("As my great-grandpappy used to say, 'There's nothing a few midgets can't solve!'"), Barnum and Bernbach launched a full-frontal attack on the school grounds and basketball courts of America, popping as many kids in the arm as was necessary (not many, really), until the brats were doing it to each other, bruising in the name of capitalism. Bernbach even managed to convince Hitchcock to include a punch-buggy sequence in *Psycho*. No one would ever forget Marilyn Monroe's wallop on the drag queen Tony Curtis in *Some Like It Hot*. And, of course, there was the short pre-movie to *Rio Bravo*, John Wayne, Dean Martin and Ricky Nelson pounding each other continually while waiting to shoot their next scene:

RN: "Red punchbuggy, no returns... wait, is that? yes! Green, John, got you again! Hey, Dean, aren't you playing? This is a hoot!"

DM: "Sure thing, Ricky."

RN: "Blue, John, no punchbacks... Pow!"

JW: "Huh..."

RN: "Oof— hey, John, watch it, I said, ow— I said no returns, I mean, ouch— hold it a second!"

"What I learned from Bill Bernbach," Barnum was fond of recounting, "was that a Great Idea could come from anywhere, Jesus, sometimes we'd just be lighting farts in the boardroom and suddenly someone would say, 'Hey, Bill, why don't we order Chinese?' And then the little delivery guy would see what we'd worked on so far and say, 'Doesn't look like so much to me,' and the next day we'd be using that in our presentation." He hissed like a Goodyear. "Good times—hey, can someone get me a beer or something?"

Roast never knew what hit him until, in the middle of the status meeting, he was escorted from the building. He'd cleared a spot in the middle of the room, was rocking back and forth on his glorious, high-tension ham hocks. And he'd already become sidetracked, sputtering and steaming about the glory days of flight, when they'd force-feed you free booze because you deserved it, and everything was so underbooked you didn't need these tiny laptops because you could set up a full fucking computer in the empty seat beside you, and the meals were prepared fresh somewhere, not created synthetically by little Star Trek replicator microwaves, and somehow they still managed to make money ("So what the hell are they doing wrong now?"). His eyes and fingers had fallen into their own private apoplectic fits: blink, blink, clench, blink...

And then suddenly:

"Excuse me, sir, I'm afraid you'll have to come with me."

Barnum had bought them out. Roast was out of a job. And Barnum himself was in charge.

Not that it made a difference to any of them. Work carried on the same as it had before. Another one of Kitchen's clients had gone from an 80% market share to 20. So they'd placed all their marbles on a product that actually lost them money to sell: an Internet service that really offered little to nothing in the way of new benefits yet cost the consumer significantly less. Bargain basement Internet service. Barnum just had a certain way of putting it: "With publicly traded companies like this, making money isn't anywhere near as important as the appearance of making money. Sure, they could charge more for it. And the increase in price would probably be worth the customers they'd lose at the bottom line. But the real money comes from the investors. You have to drive up the price of the stock. And the only way to do that is to grab as much of the market as possible. There's nothing appealing about a company who's losing the battle."

Kitchen devised an entire direct mail campaign centred around the idea of an Internet revolution, with scarred images of young people in camouflage, a slightly Asian private-schoolgirl, fiercely passionate in her stoicism, preserved with pins that read *DSL Forever*. Misworded quotes from imaginary texts like *Die Internetsfrage*. And the final lines, like fires set across the horizon:

They say the French Revolution was also started over high Internet costs.

Let them have speed!

But why just use revolution as a metaphor? Wasn't there something more tangible he could do? Here they were selling the Internet to people with millions upon millions of unrecyclable, glossy postcards. It was like continuing to tout the benefits of television via the radio. Instead, Kitchen wrote in his proposal, they'd create their own Kyoto Accord of direct marketing, establishing yearly benchmarks to reduce "celluloid waste," claiming to move to recycled materials ("Even though we're doing that already to cut costs..."), and eventually eliminating all direct mail entirely. The cost of sending emails was less than a tenth that of postcards. So they were saving money all over the place. And as everyone knew, the main goal of the project was to get people using the Internet more, especially to use their email service. Once they had them hooked into the service, they could plug them full of as much email advertising as they wanted. And they could ride the wave of PR—"The press will be all over this!"—to even more free advertising.

Barnum looked dazed. "I like what you're doing for the agency, kid. That Drano stuff? Brilliant."

"But sales went down—"

"Doesn't matter, son, you gotta look at the big picture, and I see that's what you're doing here. Who gives a shit about Drano, really? Just another replaceable client, all this is just the first step. That shit you just presented in there, though? It's radical. Pretty soon the press is going to be all over you: the socially conscious advertiser. Where did you come up with that one, tell me?"

"I just thought we have this platform and it seems like we could really make a difference sometimes—"

"You're for real, then? An altruistic copywriter? Save the Earth and shit?"

"Well..."

"Doesn't matter, kid, just makes it easier, we can *sell* that! We'll make *you* the brand! We'll have your name and face on every ad like a goddamn stamp of approval."

For Barnum, it was no longer a question of just selling products, or even landing accounts. Barnum owned most of the agencies in North America, anyway. The new game was all about selling the sell, convincing the manufacturers that advertising was more crucial to product quality—since quality was really just a perceived measure, anyway—than any sort of testing or engineering. Joe Public couldn't make up his own mind without a catchy jingle or trustworthy spokescharacter. Barnum made it clear to Kitchen from day one: The enemy was not here at home. They were abroad. International ad shops. With their nonsensical humour and sexual innuendo, their cartoonish colours and major celebrity endorsements...

"You wanna run the show, Kitchen, you gotta fill the tent, plain and simple. And it's the Asians that are tossing their money around like free Pocky sticks that have me most worried. Let me give you a little lesson in economics: there's us and there's them. Money's just a way of keeping score. Advertising's just a way of speaking to the troops. It's all about showing who's boss. You follow? You think all those Japs really give a Pokemon's ass about our American film stars? You bet they do. And more importantly they know we do, too, so they snap'm up like sushi rolls. Just a kick in my fucking pants, Kitchen, nothing else. Those actors wouldn't be caught dead peddling respectable things like liquor or home computers on this side of the divide, but the Japs are willing to shell out just a little more to protect the poor movie stars' integrity, like they had any integrity to ruin in the first place. Before you can say *me no speaky the english*, they have Brad Pitt cruising around in a Honda and Janet Jackson selling an airline Dennis Hopper pushing bath salts, I mean holy crow what's this world coming to? Do you know what Ringo Starr means in Japanese? Applesauce. Literally, his name means fucking applesauce. So he sells out his own country to peddle some Nip crap, a place where they haven't imported one Johnny American apple in over thirty years, when we've got Motts right here, and I don't need to tell you Kitchen it's a fine fucking applesauce..."

"Ringo Starr's British, I think..."

"Isn't it all the same god damn thing these days?"

"..."

"I think you'll find we won that war, son."

Using Kitchen's new credibility, Barnum produced millions of stickers reading "Brought to you by Corporate America," distributing them to schoolchildren across the country. As class projects, twelve-year-olds were supposed to identify each object they saw that wouldn't have existed without America's extensive system of factories and assembly lines, labeling it appropriately. Computers, stereos, televisions and telephones; cellphones and blackberries; Fords, Chevys and Chryslers; footballs and baseball bats; skyscrapers and hot dog carts; Mount Rushmore; the rivers, lakes and forests.

Especially the forests. Couldn't find a tree in northern California without the corporate tag on it. The forestry industry had received such a bum rap for years. But stats now showed that nearly 95% of the Earth's trees had been planted by the replenishable environment efforts of International Paper, Weyerhauser/MacMillan Bloedel or Sweden's Stora Enso. The new message? *We* are *the environment.* If it weren't for them, there would be no trees. No oxygen. Would they want to destroy themselves?

The Society of American Foresters had also renewed their attempts to get everyone buying original paper goods again. Recycling? Lord knew what it was in a prior life, where it had *been*. If anything, recycled paper was a health risk, no doubt responsible for the E.coli outbreaks that had surfaced recently across the continent. Recycled paper used in envelopes, dragged across the bumpy taste buds of every tongue in the heart of the heart of the country, it was disgusting.

The "Corporate America" stickers had practically replaced the Stars and Stripes as the nation's brand logo.

Kitchen was going to be Barnum's bald eagle.

There was a short period where he dated a girl named Veronica, which was exciting mostly because of her name. Even after they split, he'd still sit around work and dream of cartoon threesomes, an airbrushed blonde-brunette sandwich on the lip of a dollar-shaped pool. The statuesque Veronica, with not just one lazy eye but two, like a Baroque portrait, seemingly staring at you wherever you stood. Not the most appealing attribute in a face, to be sure, but she was starting her own business designing wedding dresses, which he liked because it was somewhat different and yet still involved commerce. Here was someone he could anticipate without expending too much energy. And since Gage had walked out on him, Kitchen had grown uncertain of his own esthetic tastes. He was just so thankful to be with anyone, it just didn't matter. He stared at her across the table and wondered if she were really staring back.

It was Veronica's seeming disinterest that attracted him most. He wanted to put his advertising skills to the test, to run up against a resistant audience and gradually convince her that she needed not only one of him but two. As the night wore on, however, she became distressingly easy to sell to, interested in him before he even reached the hard sell. She kept touching his hands and arms. And her words clung to his face like dew. Every angle of her body seemed set to murder him in some horrible way. She had elbows like ice picks. Her hips snarled against his like lathes. And her legs were like scythes, bow-legged, yet thankfully hidden beneath the table.

He ordered another round.

And another.

Somehow, in the midst of planning his escape, he hid in the back seat of the wrong car ("Aren't you going to sit up front with me?" she screeched over her shoulder). At the next lights, he forgot to make a run for it. And she had so many bags to carry, he simply had to help her to her front door.

Her apartment hung low to the ground, grey and filthy like the belly of an elephant. Before he knew it, her shirt was on the floor. Her back was against the stove. He was on his knees, kissing a trail from her pelvis, leading her to the couch, too excited at being intimate with anyone to wonder if he might actually feel anything for her, smelling every faint hair between her breasts. She'd found drapes at her parents' house, but she hadn't had the chance to hang them yet, so she insisted he stay between her and the window. The perverts across the street wouldn't see anything but the gnawing of his shoulder blades, possibly her face, her teeth biting into his neck, and the heels of her feet digging into the small of his back, drawing him in, and in, and in. It was also her period, so she simply rubbed her denim crotch against his until he came into the tiny recess of her belly button, her nipples so sharp they left lines across his chest.

Thank god they had absolutely nothing in common. Or they might have gone out longer. But because there were awkward silences to fill on the phone, Veronica told him he was intriguing. He thanked her, thinking, however, that he'd rather be handsome. Or interesting. And they both spent the next month thinking of ways they could end it and still look good.

He (i.e., Kitchen) had a dream about Gage that came about eight minutes into one of his half-hour naps. And later he would never be quite certain if the memories were his or just collected stills from childhood ads. Because of Gage, his life had become surrounded by PSAs. And he had no proper logo with which to resolve them.

I am Astar. A robot. I can put my arm back on. But you can't. So play safe.

But in the dream, the voice wasn't from a robot. It was a child. With eyes like igniting fuses and arms as brittle as safety regulations. She sliced her arm right off with the edge of a raw unpolished sneaker. And her efforts to fuse her limbs back together by sheer thought produced nothing but more profit for the capitalist machine Kitchen helped to fuel. He found himself defending his job to Gage in words that would have made Barnum proud:

K: "Do you ever wonder why governments and corporations give aid to third world countries?"

G: "Because protest works. Because... Because deep down we're caring human beings, it's in our nature..."

K: "The only thing that's in our nature is to grow. To. Accumulate. More. Stuff. The only reason we help those poor losers is to create more consumers for the future. It's the best form of advertising there is."

G: "And we're growing at the expense of the third world!"

K: "Hell, yes, it's called winning."

He remembered being embarrassed to tell her friends what he did for a living. He never brought it up. When they asked, he said he was a writer.

"Short stories?"

"Very short."

Fiction with strategic product placement.

Miter had set up a small desk near the jukebox at the Tagline, and he started his new Inactivist operation from there. Kitchen dropped by on his way home from work and found the art director napping amidst a sea of static enterprise. Over by the Dr Pepper saloon doors, they'd set up one of the televisions to play video games. Something that involved shooting. Everyone was talking about the weather. When Kitchen told him about the dreams he'd been having about Gage, and how he thought maybe they could make a difference, Miter ran around trying to get other people to cover his ears.

"Jesus, K, who wants to change anything? The only thing I want to change is the ability to change stuff."

The boys in the Agency's IT department joined Miter's cause almost immediately. Not that anyone noticed. Impossible to find at the best of times, they continued to wander the Agency hallways, just to keep up appearances. They had removed computers and servers from the agency, piece by piece, setting up several stations at the Tagline, and the entire west side of the bar—most of the advertising had been stripped from the walls, replaced with *Lord of the Rings* paraphernalia and anime erotica—had been turned into a near replica of the Enterprise bridge.

Miter did nothing to encourage them directly. Here was someone who simply embodied their hopes and dreams, of a four-hour workday, with endless supplies of pizza and PvP-FPS video games. And girls! Wouldn't there be girls!? A geek delegation approached him while he was unplugging photocopiers and fax machines around the office, and he barely looked up.

"We can help."

Miter just shrugged.

They were attracted to Miter partly because of his sloth, but mostly because he had moved from a passive lack of concern to an intense distrust for anything progressive. As he explained to Kitchen, Miter took them on because he finally saw, in them, what the rest of their workmates were missing: ambition to do nothing. And enough guilt from that to make them desperate.

They were also more familiar with the Internet than he was, which Miter recognized almost immediately as the tool that could make his dreams a reality. Secretly, it was the reason why those geeks had started playing with computers in the first place. Silicon terrorism. If they could understand the technology before anyone else, they would own the world. The only thing they forgot was that the ones with money could eventually just buy them out. Barnum could just dangle a salary in front of their eyes and they would give up everything they once stood for. It took Miter to give them another goal:

If they couldn't use computers to reach the top, use computers to bring everyone back down.

"The Internet is one of the biggest Inactivist inventions of this generation. It basically just lets people waste time productively. Some people might argue that it was the video game. But the Internet took video games to a completely different level. Because of online play, they want some video games to have warnings about being addictive! How awesome is that?!"

"…"

"But now people use it *for* work. So they can basically maintain an umbilical connection with the office. The Internet has been usurped, K, and if it's going to be used for evil, it's better that we don't have it at all."

Then Miter showed Kitchen the viruses, designed to take up all processing capability until every computer would have to be unplugged to stop it. One was constructed to destroy hard drives, the most basic of viruses, easily deflected by refusing to open the attached executable file. But another was really just a chain letter without any programming involved at all, a warning against a fake virus that they hoped people would spend all their time forwarding to friends, clogging up the system almost voluntarily. And a third would recreate itself indefinitely, grinding computers to a halt with these final words:

Please, remain calm. Stay where you are. Do nothing at all.

He claimed to have received the idea from the anti-protests they'd staged outside the Chinese embassy. "Remember? Those karate dudes?"

"That was just a peaceful statement. Like a sit-in. Or a hunger strike."

"Weren't they breaking furniture or something?"

"No."

"No high-pitched screams?"

"I think they were just trying to balance their own personal sense of well-being."

"It's the only real stance someone should have, K. Both feet planted firmly to either side, arms akimbo. Like a boy scout. Don't rock the boat, that's all we're trying to say…"

"…"

"Here, K, wanna do your part? Hand some of these around."

A business card. With nothing written on it at all.

It was then that he noticed the televisions again. Once they had played a ceaseless direct feed from the Cannes International Advertising Awards station. With news of the latest revues and pitches scrolling across the bottom of the screen. But now the only noise in the bar came from the periodic screech of the streetcars outside. Just like the night Gage had walked out on him, all of the televisions were off.

They ran into each other again at another of Swan's parties, too drunk to remember why they split in the first place. Kitchen was eating a bag of jujubes he'd found in a cupboard beside the fridge, dropping the black ones in potted plants around the house, and the strength of her conviction hit him like hunger.

"You know that gelatin is made with horse hooves, don't you?"

"..."

"So there's gelatin in those things, and horses were killed just so you can eat that candy?"

"..."

"It's just that you were talking about making a difference last time I saw you, and I thought maybe you were serious?"

"Mmm... pony..."

The next thing he knew, they were making out in the middle of the living room, his fingers in the loop of her belt, and her fingers splitting his pants open like a chest cavity. She kissed him as if he were a shot glass, throwing her head back and breathing in fits. His nose was locked beneath her earlobe, their temples rubbing together, his cheek burning a swath along hers.

Someone asked them to leave.

"Let's go back to my place."

Hmmm...

Outside, the winter snow surrounded them like bloated virginal debutantes. And the streets were empty of everything but repressed anger. Fist fights just waiting to happen. The landscape was such a cacophony of voices that no one knew what to do with so much white, so they turned their normal repression outward. Only the cab seemed safe, so comfortable on the expressway, protected on both sides by so many messages, Gage like a fallen quotation mark in his lap. By the time they reached her place, he was just so thankful to be in one piece that he didn't even stop to think how they had ended up together in the first place.

This was the new beginning. After she walked out on him at the Tagline, he'd convinced himself that it was over, that he was lucky to have simply slept with her. But now that he had the opportunity to do it again, he allowed thoughts of love to creep back into his head. She was the only one who understood his sense of humour. His desire to help. God, hadn't he been doing all this for her? For her! And here she was. If they could survive this minor break-up, they could survive anything. An affair. Bad breath. Even her apparent lack of things. While she was in the washroom, Kitchen inspected her Ikea picture frames, trailed a finger along the plastic milk crates full of underwear and T-shirts, the Coke can full of cigarette butts, the practically antique television set. It wasn't even a bedroom. It was just a re-purposed living room. One she was subletting—"Well, subletting is maybe a strong word…"—from a house full of friends she'd met at a protest. "They're pretty cool about it," she said. "They don't even make me pay rent, you know, they don't care at all…" But there wasn't even a door. Just an uncomfortable pullout couch without legs. And a side table with a coffee tin full of guitar picks and condoms.

Every time her head struck the couch's spine, he asked if she was alright. Eventually she told him to shut up and just keep going.

He would survive.

The first new job Barnum assigned him was for High Liner Frozen Foods. With partial funding from the Nova Scotian company, some scientist at NASA had succeeded in growing fish muscle in a "nutrient-rich vat." And it was already being touted as one of the most important discoveries of the new century. It had also opened an entirely new chapter in the abortion debate. Animal rights activists questioned when these pieces of flesh became actual fish. Was it not possible that the hunks in question felt pain or could anticipate their own ends? At what point did the fish become infused with a soul? Certainly there were some groups that refused to believe animals had any souls at all. But they were all unanimous in their agreement that the CEO of a frozen fish plant should not be playing god, particularly when he portrayed himself as such a friend to children ("Have you ever been to sea, Billy?"). Kids were so impressionable, liable to take another person's word as truth without really questioning its veracity or bias. Did they not owe it to the global community to provide food alternatives that were actually food?

"Global community—Jesus Christ." The bearded Captain High Liner was forced to hire Barnum as a PR consultant, and advertising's *enfant terrible* took the podium like a randy dog. "You people have to understand that there's nothing wrong with what we're doing here. This here's just an honest fisherman trying to make an honest living. Don't let the suit fool you, this one is as salty as they come. And the truth of the matter is this could save you hippies having to slaughter animals for food."

Liner stepped awkwardly forward. "Well, first of all, I'd just like to point out that the Captain is just a character I play in the commercials, I don't normally speak like a pirate or anything...But secondly, my team and I have been performing these tests for years now, and I can honestly say that our reconstituted fish product contains all the nutrients you would expect to find in fish without any harmful side effects...or the bones..."

And Barnum leaned forward into the microphone. "She makes a mean fish-stick, too. Arrr!"

Kitchen was supposed to write the first campaign. Something edgy that would make people take notice and forget that it wasn't real food. He figured they could burn the sweepstakes message right on to the fish sticks. *Bite me*. He was sure Gage could help him. But Gage was upset not only about this, but also over the other so-called "frankenfoods" they were developing: inserting salmon genes into Washington apples to prevent them from bruising, crossing tomatoes with peanuts to give them more protein, injecting reptile DNA into kiwi vines to make the fruit more hairless and palatable...

"Seriously, Kitchen, there are some very practical issues involved in this kind of stuff, like, in the salmon case? Some people don't eat salmon cos they're vegetarian, right? But my dad doesn't eat salmon cos he's deathly allergic, and if there's no labelling requirement then how does he know not to eat it?" She motioned to the bartender for another glass of wine. "When his throat swells up and he can't breathe and has to be rushed to the hospital for a shot of something or other to open his windpipe, and hopefully he doesn't asphyxiate before he gets there, well, how does he know it's because of the slice of apple pie he had after dinner? Or even the huge glass of milk, holy, don't get me started on that Bovine Growth Hormone crap..."

"But couldn't this solve so many problems? Space exploration is obviously the first, but what about world hunger?"

"Hunger has nothing to do with food, Kitchen, it's all about allocation—"

"Which is why we need more resilient food in the first place, so it doesn't rot before it gets to Africa or whatever..."

"So help them farm their own land, I'm sure every child on Planet Earth has a birthright to consume fishcakes and spaghetti for lunch every Friday, but I also think fish hunks may have some trouble staying fresh while we ship them to Ethiopia. Maybe I'm wrong, though. Maybe after they grow it, they'll freeze-dry it and drop it in little care packages from airplanes to the starving masses below. Along with bottles of anemic baby formula, and a pile of Gideon Bibles. Hip, hip..."

"But these are like plants, Gage, couldn't we just sell them like Chia Pets? You buy a little clay fish, and an eyedropper of fetal bovine serum, and then just carve the shit off as needed! No shipping necessary."

"..."

"..."

"..."

Despite the plunging temperatures, labour solidarity was wet and glistening beneath the noonday sun. Local 181 (which, in truth, did not exist and was only a front for one of Barnum's latest guerilla marketing squadrons, named after Pepsi's street address) had organized a walkout at the 7UP bottling facility on the outskirts of the City, citing better working conditions as one of the stipulations of their new contract. They wanted a pension plan that would allow them to retire before the age of sixty-two without penalties; the microwave in the lounge could barely heat a cup of coffee in under five minutes; and they all required a new health plan to cover things like high cholesterol treatments due to rampant obesity, anti-depression medication, lithium poisoning—

"Oh, god," the spokesperson for Cadbury (who'd long ago purchased one of America's oldest soft drinks, along with Dr Pepper and Hires) told the press. "For the last time, we don't use lithium in our products any more."

Of course, it was just one of many demands, slogans burned into memory by countless placards and fliers. Truth be told, most of the workers probably would have given up the pay raise if they could just get that microwave. Meanwhile, they spent $4/cup on the store-bought chi-chi beans, handed it out around the crackling trash cans. They mopped their brows with the polyester sleeves of their skin-tight parkas. They took turns warming up the engines of their cars. They lit up their cigarettes (*Don't believe it... You're still Kool*) and ate homemade-looking sandwiches from the convenience store around the corner. Effort was so difficult sometimes. Especially when the winters in this place hung on like leftovers, frozen and burnt, so distasteful, barely connected with the magical dustings of the fall, when the first flakes melted almost instantly on the tongues of the recess rank and file—because somehow the pollution didn't seem to effect the snow like it did the rain?!—and they could all still convince themselves this was as bad as it would ever get. There wasn't even anything to talk about any more. Except the dwindling hope of spring. The Olympics (seemed like all the hockey players at the Winter Olympics were European this time around, even the ones playing for Canada and the US, the Nike swoosh riding their last names like ornate umlauts). Or that bum who'd frozen to death on the west side, who'd buried herself in a dumpster to conserve heat, and wasn't found until the next garbage day, wrapped in discarded scarves she'd found near bus shelters, arms like sled rails, blue as a failing spark.

Of course, this brought on the usual comments about global warming, ozone, fashion.

Someone brought up the idea of a weather-control dome.

Miter saw the strike as a counterattack. They were on to him. What had he been thinking with the Internet? He'd just created a mild annoyance. Couldn't even get arrested. So he began to pursue his goals through more overt machinations and blatant aggression. Outside the 7UP gates, Miter had surrounded himself with an army of slackers, people Kitchen had never seen before, except Swan, the IT boys, and a few suits from the account side, all representing Miter's great Call to Inaction. They encircled the stunned bottlers with signs of their own, significantly larger and bolder (manufactured by Swan's production crew at the Agency), featuring nothing but a large red circle with a line through it.

No more signs.

Their words were loud and rhythmic.

"Shouting slogans doesn't work! Shouting slogans doesn't work!"

For a moment, there was a standoff. The bottlers seemed unsure of how to proceed.

Then they rolled up their sleeves and started forward.

It was the vegetarians who forced McDonald's to switch from frying with beef tallow to vegetable oil, changing the flavour and texture of their fries forever. There was a lawsuit. There was emotional distress (another lawsuit). And in the end, the fast food giant was forced to change their age-old recipe, passed down from clown father to clown son until Ronald turned his great-grandfather's dream into reality.

But the fries didn't taste the same, and McDonald's was forced to come up with some other option. The growing number of vegetarians was distressing, to be sure. But if they could stop the tide there, before people moved completely into veganism, then there was hope. "Gee," McDonald said to the other board members. "We don't have to kill the cows to get at that cellulite gold. All those helplessly overweight cattle... challenged by the threat of diabetes and heart disease... sleep apnea... gout... Those cows need our help, and by golly, we're going to give it to them."

Animal fat harvested completely by liposuction.

It was the second time around that Kitchen learned so much about Gage. She had some pretty crazy ideas about animals, for one thing. He'd been so busy falling in love the first time that he'd barely paid attention, so was stunned when he bragged to her about Barnum's latest plan ("We'll call it *FATTLE!*, with a goddamn trademark on the exclamation point!"), and she made it sound bad!

"But you're missing the whole point, Gage, this isn't animal *testing*, it's animal *improving*... And the best part is it's totally safe, no chance of getting mad cow disease or anything, McDonald's has its own closed herd, and—"

"Are you joking? Can you seriously sit there in front of me and tell me you're not joking, like, wow, I have to let the guys in on this one, cos you're not joking, are you? Kitchen! If you can't just see it, how can I ever hope to explain it to you?"

He began to wonder if she were really who she said she was. What if she'd just used the whole "concern for animals and the environment" thing to sell herself to him?

Even her outward cries of passion ("Hear her?" one of her roommates replied when prodded, "guy, it's like she's in my room with me, shit, I'm running out of hand cream!") began to seem disingenuous.

Was this the person he hoped to understand?

It was then that he really started watching her, picking through the garbage for neglected compostables, making sure the recycling actually made it to the curb. Her bookshelves, he began to notice, seemed strangely settled. Not full of the texts he'd expected to find: Rachel Carson's *Silent Spring*. Something by David Suzuki. *The Anarchist Cookbook*. *The Moosewood Cookbook*. Instead? Math books. Thick with diagrams and digits; triangles that didn't surround toxic symbols like rubber bumper car fenders; circles that were not Venn diagrams. When she came back from the Chinese grocer, he was still leafing through it.

"I thought you were an environmental studies major?"

"What gave you that idea? Wow, I mean, that's just how I live, like, I'm studying trigonometry."

"There's a whole degree in performing emergency throat surgery?"

Their whole relationship was a lie.

He was sure he could look past it. After all, wasn't love all about ignoring the aspects of a person you didn't like or understand? And this whole thing was his cause, not hers. If she wasn't as committed to it as he was, then so be it. He was sure he could bring her around. The main issue was that she had trouble making commitments. Math was her third major in as many years. She grew bored in chess. And any resolution she made to get back in shape was met with severe internal indifference. In the mornings, when his eyes snapped open without the shrill encouragement of her alarm clock, she burrowed deeper into sleep, saliva like a slug along the yellow-tinged pillowcases, her face blotchy and red and traced with the maps of the bunched sheets' imaginary landscapes. Kitchen kissed her shoulder, stared down at her as loudly as possible, slid a finger between her legs…

"Look, don't make me feel guilty, okay?"

"Wasn't this your idea?"

So, she'd decided to start with flossing, figuring this was something manageable. But there never seemed to be any time. She was so tired before going to bed. And in the mornings her jaw was sore from chronic grinding.

"Maybe you should start with something smaller," he suggested.

Barnum had Kitchen doing undercover work to see how they could more easily reach "today's youth." About all he deduced was that elementary kids swore like truckers on fire:

"Throw the fucking ball!"

"Suck me!"

"Wait up, you fucking dickwad!"

And the seesaw came down with a crash that sent one little girl sprawling and the rest of them spastic with malevolent sniggers.

"Ow! My fucking cunt!"

The school board had passed some kind of ruling that they wouldn't allow education to be bought by huge corporations. They'd removed all pop machines from the cafeteria. The annual sale of overpriced chocolate bars was cancelled altogether. There was essentially no way advertisers could reach them inside school walls (when their minds were being occasionally propped open by sudden bouts of interest) outside of inserting ads directly into their Game Boys. So Barnum's plan was to buy entire schoolyards by sponsoring only the coolest kids. Just like they did with professional athletes. "Really," Barnum slithered softly through the presentation, "you guys are spending millions to get one major basketball star to wear your sneakers. Just think of how many kids we can get for that! They gotta cost what—? Couple hundred max? Pick the three or four coolest kids in each school and you're *still* saving money..."

Barnum called it *formative advertising*.

But Gage wasn't excited about this one either, which was when Kitchen accused her of being contrary on purpose. And not very supportive, if she wanted to know. As if nothing he did was any good. Why did she have to hate his friends so much? First Miter. Now Barnum.

"Listen to yourself, Kitchen, you're like his little monkey—"

"Geezus, why can't you just pat me on the back and say, 'Job well done,' every once in a while? Your negative attitude, it's like, whoa..."

"But you're infringing on the rights of defenceless children!"

"We're helping poor kids put something away for university!"

In the end, Kitchen and Gage just failed to live up to each other's dreams. They took a bath together because they decided it would be sexy, then discovered it was just uncomfortable. She couldn't straddle wide enough to get him inside her. The concavity of her bend made him entirely too convex. Someone had to slouch low enough to allow for the faucet. And then everything she did seemed like the blunt dig of plated chrome between the tension of his overworked shoulder blades.

Her views were so clouded lately, so influenced by her roommates. The war against terrorism was really about oil? Globalization was a problem? Because he wanted them to like him, he entertained her roommates with all the best stories he knew, how Barnum was changing the world with his innovative approaches: the lithium hoax, the fish plants, the liposuctioned fat...

And the whole room stared back at him in silence.

When her friends began to mock her (how could she really be *for* the people if she wasn't actually one of them?), she became even more distant. When Kitchen pointed out a clever billboard for a perfume depicting a supermodel posing as a First Nations priestess ("Or something voodoo, I'm not sure..."), she pretended to be disgusted. And when she claimed she wasn't running any more because her sneakers had been made in sweat shops and she didn't want to be a mobile billboard like those poor kids he was exploiting—

"Can't you see you're just spouting back a bunch of useless rhetoric, Gage, I mean, I can see it for what it is, I'm sure you can too..."

"You're demeaning a cause I believe in."

"Believe in? Since when does helping people have anything to do with belief?" They had the nerve to judge him when he had the proof of results behind him? What was the last thing they had seen accomplished with marches and petitions? If they wanted to see people who weren't doing enough, maybe they should look at themselves first. They had no scope. Their inclination to improve things was limited by their frustrating spirit of rebellion. It was easy to rely on anger when you were younger. But anger, as a fuel, was fast burning. He saw them all working behind desks for the government in five years, filing and budgeting, power lunching; and he told Gage so in as many words.

Gage told him to fuck off.

"Remember when we first met? You were so worked up about the homeless and whatever, what happened to that? Well, why couldn't we get companies to sponsor the burials? Huh? Cemeteries are the last untapped media source. We could convince major corporations to purchase bulk plots in some of the world's more popular graveyards, set up flower kiosks all around the perimeter, and then create a PR campaign to give the poor losers a decent send-off. For a few thousands bucks, they'd get eternal space on a—"

"They'd get what?"

"Eternal space...?"

"I just don't understand this fascination with money and selling, it's like you don't care what you put into people's hands. The food... those strikers... You could be convincing them to drink poison, and, no wait, just listen for a second—"

"That's a bit of an exaggeration, Gage, I mean, there's really no point in killing off your customers just for one sale—"

"Maybe you should just quit advertising and join us on a protest..."

"What are you talking about? Advertising is the *voice* of protest! You think these groups could ever be heard without the advertising strength we're providing them? Without Barnum, these people are trees falling in the forest. Or, what was it that kid called me? Mouthless faces or something? So what if we're getting our client's name out there in the process, we're still promoting a good cause at the same time—"

"But they're so totally opposite!"

"How can you even think that, I mean, what did you think those strikers wanted? All those guys want is to keep their jobs. And if we can build the strength of our American brands over the international competition, if we can make the company more successful and therefore bigger, there's going to be more jobs, more job security. You know? Their problem with globalization isn't unsafe working conditions in South America or Asia, it's that lower standards in South America and Asia enable those places to steal our jobs. So screw South America and Asia, Gage, with their Pocky sticks, their Brazilian Guaraná. Screw Orangina and Schweppes, too!"

"Some of us just want to make the world a better place."

"Sure we do. And hopefully some day the rest of world will see things the way we see them."

"We?"

The next spring, there were no leaves on the trees at all. The end of that winter had brought them all four seasons every week, repeated over and over within the space of days. The repeated death of fall. Those sandpaper winter breezes. The sweating sidewalks of spring, the City waking with alcoholic nightmares and shakes. Dark morning spots of perspiration. It was all you could do just to concentrate on not sweating too much. Then, suddenly, the windows once again seemed insufficient to hold back the chill. No one left the house at all. Any exposed buds were shattered from their perches, or gnawed off by confused squirrels. Finally the plant world just said, "Fuck it," and packed it all in.

No one was sure how to react. But the supermarkets took no chances. Both grocery stores and drugstores had started stocking their razor blades at or behind the cash registers. There had been a rash of suicides, major depressives tearing open a pack of Gillettes in aisle three and hemorrhaging all over the soap, the condoms, the blood pressure machine. It was similar to Walmart's decision to put guns and ammunition at opposite ends of the store. No need to tempt the droopy-faced buggers.

Of course, that kind of "application" (the word they used in the official press releases) was never good for sales. It was certainly never condoned. For a while they considered adding disclaimers to the packaging: *Not to be used in any life-altering decisions*. But they didn't want to destroy the illusion that a clean-shaven face could dramatically improve your love life. So the new store placement seemed the most effective way to go.

Also, the weather caused the price of fruits and vegetables in grocery store chains to skyrocket. Only on the streets did it start to drop. There were theories that the mom and pops had formed some sort of secret cabal against the major supermarkets, that there was, perhaps, a secret underground farm, located possibly in the mountains of the northwest but not necessarily, where cost-effective American-grown vegetables could be picked year round, under the delicious synthetic sunshine of thousands of tanning beds, everything funded by the "take a penny leave a penny" dishes at the foot of each outdated cash register.

Here were the *real* pushers of genetically produced produce. But Kitchen wasn't buying it. The reduced prices were hardly a selling point when the early morning frosts seemed to destroy everything by noon from the inside out. Firm, perfectly yellowed lemons were soft and brown at the epicentre. The skins of the peppers were soft and elderly. The herbs tasted like dirt. Plus, how could you know the quality of one of those little shops when they never took the time to show you on television? The supermarkets were fresh obsessed. They were fresh to your family. Fresh from their table to yours. Fresh was their middle name.

So Kitchen bought some more exotic fruit ("The produce guy called them 'leather kiwis.'"), and brought them to Miter in the hospital. After most of the Inactivists refused to fight back, the strikers lost it, and brought their bottles down hard. Miter had broken several ribs. And a glass cut along his forearm had severed the flexor tendon. The doctors were pretty sure he'd never have full use of it again. But it had done nothing to dissuade him. The lawsuit money, he was being told, would probably support him for the rest of his life. Now he could afford to do nothing forever.

"Of course, you're the real inactivist, K, only you keep fighting it. You spend all your time trying to help people. Or pretending you're someone else to impress a girl. At the most, you end up where you started. At the worst, you get hurt. You're no better off than you were when you started, and all you really had to do was just sit there, and you would have accomplished the same thing."

And maybe Miter was right. Was it worth spending all this effort for several years of delusive emotions and then sudden epileptic heartbreak?

The best thing to do was not try at all.

"Oh, shut up!" Barnum pulled his great-grandpappy's top hat down over his eyes. "You think I got anywhere in this world by giving up? Shit, no, we each have the chance to make a difference. Just most people squander that chance. And shut up already about that girl. Emotions can't be fooled. It's not like you just believed you were happy because you thought you were in love. You *were* happy. And if you want anything back, you have to go get it. Anything you want is worth fighting for..."

Everything at the Agency was dark. As Miter had already anticipated, his victory there was easy and hollow. Extended lunches turned into open hours. Soon everyone was pretending to work from home. Then they stopped pretending.

But Barnum was seated at his desk behind a congregation of crumpled paper. Advertising's wunderkind. Down but not out. Whenever he felt writer's block setting in, he changed his socks, ate a chocolate bar, laid down on the floor, anything that might change his luck. Another chair, perhaps. He'd tried them all, every castered straight-back and stool in the Agency. And the hallway outside his office was polluted with the discards.

Barnum's attempt to save McDonald's through live bovine lipid extraction fell on deaf ears. Consumers didn't buy it for a second. As soon as the ads hit the airwaves (herds of cows in line to get nose jobs and udder augmentations), there was an immediate counter-campaign launched by an independent group of activists, a barbaric animation with cows as machines, taking food in one end and having fat sucked out the other. It was one of Barnum's first real failures as an advertiser ("Someone must have tipped them off…"), but more importantly, McDonald's sales continued to plummet. That winter they posted their first quarterly loss ever. And investors shuddered at thoughts of capitalist downfall.

McDonald's went back to the drawing board. Maybe the problem was globalization on a much simpler scale? What if all this constant cultural exchange (something they'd positioned themselves against from the beginning, in a series of war time ads that featured underweight Vietnamese soldiers brandishing chopsticks like objects of torture over the disembowelled intestines of fallen G.I.s) had poisoned the North American palate, making it impossible to taste anything but spices and fish? What was once a home-style burger of particular note had developed into a bland piece of cardboard stuffed between two doughy carbohydrate repositories. Their french fries were just starchy potatoes without sesame seeds or cayenne. Someone suggested a complete menu overhaul. And they came to Barnum to position it.

Barnum wouldn't let them. "If we can't stick by a good old-fashioned American dream," he practically bawled to the Board, "then what good is this thing we call Freedom? Ronald, what would your grandfather say to changing his original recipe by even one ounce of 100% beef? What we need, ladies and gentlemen, is something to go that extra step." If these people were just against incorporation in general, what would they listen to? What did they need more than anything to continue living the way they did? The answer was out there. He was sure of it. He'd left the meeting alone, and headed back to the Agency to sit with his three-ring circus of thoughts, to jump through all the hoops of creativity until he could re-emerge victorious.

This was the game. The set of rules by which Barnum measured each day of his life.

And he was planning on winning it.

"If we're not happy, Kitchen, we're just not trying hard enough."

Kitchen was staring at the computer screen over Barnum's shoulder:

Please, remain calm. Stay where you are. Do nothing at all.

Please, remain calm. Stay where you are. Do nothing at all.

Please, remain calm. Stay where you are. Do nothing at all...

epilogue.

Refreshments for the WTO protesters were provided by PepsiCo. Orders straight from top pop headquarters in Purchase (no joke), New York. Fifty flats of the big red, white and blue, in six-packs, held together only by polystyrene strappers (i.e., "Hi-Cones," can cozies, fishnets) and the desire for change. Would it be enough? Was the caffeine/sugar dosage sufficient to maintain those late night vigils, wedged behind the alley dumpsters concealing miniature cans of spray paint, praying to god, no, wait, something else, surely, but praying nevertheless, that the dogs would pass by again? Someone had said the dogs were poisonous, but no one had survived even the initial serration of those purebred carnassials. If it were true (and wasn't that how the dogs were sold? through Monsanto's new Roundup® Canine Division? alongside their own cure-all mithridate?), the systemic toxin traces were washed away with the blood and corpses by the City's firehoses, or swept into waste management trucks, bearing huge billings for Pampers, In-Sink-Erator garbage disposals, and in two delicious puns, Jenny Craig and the Nintendo Game Cube.

For the caffeine intolerant? A little Sierra Mist, of course. Named after the Sierra Club environmental group to reinforce its crisp, clean flavour-image. And as a token of appreciation, just for showing up goddammit, they were given drawstring pro-fleece pullovers from the Gap, their low slung, deep kangaroo pouches filled with peaceful things like flowers and doves, Old Navy face kerchiefs, Banana Republic gas masks, Kodak instant cameras to capture the precious memories, thank you, thank you, as they dismounted the bus from Ass Scratch, Ohio; Buttfuck,

Saskatchewan; Nowhere, New Hampshire ("Live free or die, dude!"). Even a few from Necedah. Not to mention the winners in PepsiCo's "Who Wants to be a Protester?" contest. The City welcomed them with incense canisters, and the foreign indignantaries recognized the effort their hosts were making—even if it were a little misplaced—by coughing and sneezing, weeping openly. It was the curse of the younger generation—making them so allergic to even the tiniest bit of perfume. But they recognized the warm intent, and some of those tears were more emotional than reactionary.

When the protesters fell back, Gatorade was there to pick them up. "Is it in you?" their leaders shouted through red and blue branded megaphones. "IS IT IN YOU?!" Brought to a frenzy by so much sugar and electrolytes, the love-all cloy of marijuana, and the sight of so many discarded bags of Lay's and Doritos (America's best-selling snack food practically since its inception), the protesters moved forward with renewed determination, mounted fences and lampposts. Levi's opened their windows with bricks and newspaper boxes, held a clearance sale at prices you would not believe, and pretty soon everybody was kickboxing. Or breakdancing. From the angles they showed it on television, it was often hard to tell. Two hairboys were fighting over the last pair of 26 longs, which was ridiculous, when you thought about it, since there was another Levi's not too far away, and the night manager, who'd been in the back studying for her grade 12 math exam when the surprise sale started, was already on the phone to them asking for assistance ("Please...help..."). Everybody would get what he or she wanted. It was just a matter of patience.

Only the police seemed against this form of free enterprise. So far, only the New York fire department had managed to market itself properly as a civil entity, had even opened up FDNY outlets in all the major centres. But the rest of the country's heat had recently decided to trademark the no-name POLICE and FIRE DEPARTMENT logos, were planning on coming out with their own line of blue jeans under the label Bulletproof™, and they descended on the denim desperados with all the force available to them. The two police phalanxes, dressed in unadorned bruise-blue and char-black, formed a single line twelve men deep. Faceless. One enterprising youth on the side of the "consumers" had fashioned a crude Molotov cocktail from his empty soda can. The carbonated incendiary arced almost gracefully over the heads of the local peace-keeping force. Ripped apart by the resultant blast, small shards of blue aluminum shrapnel embedded themselves in the masks, vests and steel-toed boots of the municipal soldiers. One man went down with the patriotic Pepsi ball jutting like a gigantic stud from the one exposed piece of skin below his ear. His partner, cradling the dying man's head in his lap, raised his fists to heaven and thanked god he'd at least died defending the rights of their stockholders!

It was the shot Trapeza led with on the six o'clock, live at the scene, her Motorola held close like a war hero ("In this case, I guess you'd say Pepsi Cola really did hit the spot..."). But it was unlikely the rallies would take the same precedence tomorrow. Only hours into the protest and the journalists had already picked the newsworthy carcass clean. Viewers were getting bored with the same old shots, these riots, this rock throwing and spray painting, girls with very long hair or very short hair beside boys with very long hair or very short hair, only with glasses, sometimes with hats, or masks. The viewers were tuning more often to public broadcasting, who at least could be counted on for nature shows, where there was always the threat of impending death, or searing pain, with the occasional British sitcom. So a small brigade of elite associate producers were sent out to meet clandestinely with the representatives from Greenpeace and Oxfam, the International Brotherhood of Teamsters, the Anarchist Action Collective and the Continental Direct Action Network.

"If you want the coverage, guy, you gotta give us something more we can use? *Capice*? Are we understanding each other?"

"Cool, man, what about, like, a nude march down the main drag, you know, to really draw attention to freedom?"

"It's a start."

Barnum, of course, was behind everything (even, would it be known, Trapeza's story assignments). Only weeks prior, he'd puffed himself up in front of the head PepsiCo honchos, tightened his vocal chords, and barkerized about the future of guerilla advertising:

"Ladies and gentlemen, you can't buy better publicity than this. Not with hot air balloons. Not with dancing bears. Not with bearded ladies..." Just picturing those dancing bears almost made Barnum lose track of his pitch, imagining them humping on the ridge of a giant Pepsi ball. Heck, he knew this was different. He could see they were weary to even try it. But so was the "Entertainment Marketing" strategy of 1985, when they hired Lionel Richie and Michael J. Fox ("People *believe* Canadians, doesn't matter if they know they're Canadian or not...") to star in sixty or ninety minute spots, several of them serialized, touting the benefits of Diet Pepsi as a weight-loss alternative, sexual expedient and celebrity catalyst. And *that* worked like a frosted lucky charm on the consumerist zeitgeist of the eighties. "But it was all up hill, even then, let me tell you. Had to really sell them on Richie. 'Heck,' they said, 'no one's going to drink a soda flogged by a black man, it just ain't natural!' And I said, 'I'll give you natural! Show me one kid in this country that doesn't know the words to the *Ghostbusters* theme song and I'll show you a kid who gets beat up at recess every day. That kid can't even drink Pepsi anyway cos of his broken jaw. I admit I don't know everything about what goes on in the minds of kids these days. But I do know one thing, gentlemen, plain and simple.

"'Who you gonna call? Lionel Richie.'"

Barnum was popping off exclamation points like champagne corks, already celebrating the landing of another major client. "This here's the *new* celebrity! These masked patriots are the heroes of every child in this nation, goddammit, and I won't rest until every one of those homemade bombs in those hot little hands has a Pepsi logo flying right off it!"

Of course, there were some legal issues. Could the company be sued for any damage caused using their products? Could they be persecuted under the new USA Patriot Act (H.R. 3162) for supplying home-soil terrorists? Barnum would have none of this naysaying. Hadn't Pepsi always been at the forefront of change? For *good*? "We gave them the two-litre plastic, for crying out loud. Am I right? Huh? Forget the Next Generation, how about the Next Revolution? How about the Brave Next World?!"

In Barnum's Brave New Greatest Show on Earth, advertising ruled. Did the government think they could run this place without it? It won them the elections. It kept the economy pulsing. Pumping. Humping! (He thrust his pelvis like a hinged woodpecker.) Despite all the fuss they raised about Microsoft's software monopoly in the antitrust lawsuit, laying sanctions against Bill Gates that he covered with his own cheque book, what it all came down to was that the Americans now owned a piece of nearly every computer in the world. They controlled the medium, controlled the way people perceived things, the way they communicated. Microsoft Word alone was the most subversive agent of the ongoing American Revolution. Did they think those Brits and Canadians could last much longer spelling words like *colour* and *honour* with the defaults on their spellcheckers set to *English (United States)*? And what was up with the extra *i* in the British *aluminium*? America was all about brevity, getting to the point, making ends meet. Productivity had been the elected President for more than two hundred years running. And advertising was the State of the God Damned Union!